T0146811

INJURED
Dove

Janet Moller

authorHOUSE®

AuthorHouse™ UK
1663 Liberty Drive
Bloomington, IN 47403 USA
www.authorhouse.co.uk
Phone: 0800.197.4150

Published by AuthorHouse 06/14/2016

ISBN: 978-1-5246-3559-6 (sc)
ISBN: 978-1-5246-3560-2 (hc)
ISBN: 978-1-5246-3558-9 (e)

Library of Congress Control Number: 2016909709

Print information available on the last page.

Chapter One

Penny stared through the window, horror and bewilderment mounting in ever increasing waves throughout her body, causing uncontrollable trembling.

Doctor Michael Weston, her soon- to- be- married fiancé, was passionately kissing Jane Radcliffe, her best friend since childhood.

Waves of nausea washed over the nurse and she staggered away from the window, groping for the fire escape exit, desperate to flee the nightmarish scene playing out in the so-called privacy of the treatment room.

Frantic to get out of the hospital and into fresh air, she rushed down the stairs to the ground floor and, with a resounding crash, hurled open the doors, running blindly along the path bordering the entrance to Accident and Emergency, oblivious to the curious stares of paramedics driving up in an ambulance.

On reaching the Garden of Rest, the distraught nurse collapsed onto a wooden seat nestled between two large oak trees. Shuddering uncontrollably, tears flowing unchecked, she pulled her knees up to her chest and wrapping trembling arms around her legs, hugged herself tightly; rocking to and fro, just like she did as a child when upset, but this time comfort wasn't forthcoming.

"Am I blind, or stupid, or both?" she hissed through clenched teeth.

Confusion and betrayal screamed unrelentingly within her head.

"I know Michael's been edgy lately. I put it down to nerves. Our wedding's only two months away. Our wedding! I guess that won't be happening anymore," and tears welled up again.

"But Jane! How could Jane do this to me? We've been friends forever. We went to primary school together, for heavens sake. We even opted doing our nursing training at the same hospital because we didn't want to be apart. How could she betray me like this?"

But recent incidents manoeuvred their way to the forefront of Penny's tormented mind; incidents not making any sense at the time but now were oh so painfully clear. Jane finding excuses for not joining her and Michael for coffee or whatever, Michael doing a disappearing act if Jane walked into the room. She'd worried they'd taken a strong dislike to each other for some reason and this was going to upset the wedding plans, Jane being her chief bridesmaid. A strong dislike! What a sick joke.

"And to think I asked both of them if there was a problem," she whispered in agony. "Why was my best friend avoiding my husband to be? Why was Michael treating Jane as though she had the plague? Why didn't they have the guts to tell me? How cowardly is that?"

She winced as unbidden memories flooded her brain of the first time she met the man who meant everything to her.

There'd been an appalling road traffic accident involving two cars colliding head on. It was Penny's first day working in Accident and Emergency and she felt her stomach knot with nervousness on hearing the ambulances, sirens blaring, squeal through the gates of the hospital with the injured. Several of the victims were teenagers out on a joy ride ending in mangled metal and shattered bodies. She wondered how she'd cope with such a baptism of fire.

But Michael had been her knight in shining armour. He'd seen this young nurse momentarily paralysed by the enormity of the situation, and then saw her square her shoulders and march into the affray. He knew she was terrified, but she kept her head and did everything expected of her.

The doctor organised the workload making sure Penny became his assistant, and soon realised he was working with a born nurse.

Some people go into nursing just to have a job. Others, like Penny, are born to care, it's their vocation, and he verified this once the crisis was over and her shift had ended.

When Penny emerged from the nurses' change room, he wasted no time in asking her to join him for a drink at the local pub, an old coaching inn within walking distance from the hospital.

Seated in the cosy snug at the Green Coachman, Penny told the doctor she knew what she wanted to do with her life when only three years old. Her parents had bought her a nurse's outfit for Christmas and that was it. She announced to her mother her dream of becoming a nurse and her resolve had never changed.

Captivated by this softly spoken, gentle creature sitting opposite him, Michael found her stunningly attractive, with the most amazing eyes he'd ever seen, but Penny appeared completely unaware of her beauty. Determined to get to know her better, the young doctor asked her out on a second date.

Penny felt the magnetism of a kindred soul, so gladly accepted. His enthusiasm for his chosen career and the empathy he felt for his patients attracted her immensely. It also helped he was very good to look at. Her fingers longed to weave their way through his thick, brown wavy hair whilst his first kiss made her lips and body yearn for more. It wasn't long before she was head over heels in love with him, and he professed the same feelings for her. Yes, call it a whirlwind romance. Nevertheless, Penny didn't hesitate accepting Michael's proposal on Valentines Day, during an intimate dinner at an upmarket restaurant.

Her parents were delighted, especially her mother who'd always fancied having a doctor as a son in law.

So, how did such a perfect union go wrong? What did Jane have that Penny was lacking?

Sure, her friend was attractive to look at, and possessed a great personality as well as a gift for making people laugh.

Is that it? thought Penny. *Am I too serious, no fun to be with? But why didn't Michael say anything? Surely he wasn't prepared to go ahead with our marriage knowing he has feelings for somebody else? Would he have told me before the wedding? Is it as simple as him falling out of love with me?*

Tears welled up again and trickled down her face. Her world had ended, happiness and contentment destroyed in one fell swoop, replaced with anguish and despair. Her life would never be the same.

Dragging herself to the present, she looked despondently at her watch and knew she had to go back to the hospital to finish her shift.

Sister Morris would be on the warpath if she didn't get to the ward pretty quickly.

But how to face Jane? Should she make out she hadn't seen anything, or should she confront her with the evidence and demand an explanation?

No, not yet. I'm too upset and emotional. I'll end up making a fool of myself and I'm not prepared to do that. I need to salvage some of my pride.

So, just before entering the ward, Penny took a deep breath and lifted her head high, the smile on her face hiding a heart shattered into tiny pieces.

The nurse had no idea how she spoke to Jane as naturally as she did when her erstwhile friend asked where she'd been.

"I took a detour through the Garden of Rest after dropping off the lab specimens. Why? Is sister looking for me?"

"No, not sister, Mrs. Otis."

"Is she back from recovery already? Her operation went well then," and Penny turned away, glad of the excuse to terminate the conversation.

The least I should get is an Oscar for Best Female Actress, she thought, whilst making Mrs. Otis as comfortable as possible after having a hernia operation that morning. She reminded Penny of her beloved grandmother, so an extra bit of T.L.C. was in order.

The interminable shift finally ended, and making an excuse to Jane not to walk with her to the car park, Penny hurried to her car, and was driving out of the driveway before Jane had even left the hospital.

The girls shared a flat together, but Jane had told Penny she'd made arrangements to visit her parents that afternoon. At least, that's what she said. But was it true, or was she meeting Michael? He'd said he'd lectures to attend.

Penny let herself into the flat, rushed to her bedroom, locked the door and flung herself onto the bed.

And then she sobbed and sobbed until finally, there were no more tears left. She felt exhausted but strangely calm, almost robotic, when walking to the bathroom to wash her face in cold water. Looking in the mirror, she saw a stranger staring back; eyes lifeless, cold and unfathomable.

They were still beautiful. In fact, it was the one feature Penny actually liked about her face, the rest she thought uninteresting, but not her eyes. No, they were an amazing violet blue colour, enhanced by thick black, curving eyelashes and flawlessly sculptured eyebrows, causing envy amongst Penny's friends who battled with curling tongs, mascara and tweezers. Michael had always said he longed to spend the rest of his life just looking into her eyes, *but Michael is no longer part of my life, and Michael was lying*, thought Penny, and laid a cold, wet flannel over her face to help erase the evidence of her weeping.

A plan formed in her mind.

She would give Michael his freedom, and at the same time, salvage a remnant of pride. She would tell him she'd made a terrible mistake and that she didn't love him anymore. She was calling the wedding off and please would he forgive her but she just couldn't go through with it. And surely it was better to do it now rather than find out the marriage was a huge mistake after the wedding vows had been taken?

She stared at her refection for a long moment, and then spoke out loud. "Will I be able to keep up the pretence? I must. I refuse having anybody pity and feel sorry for me as the scorned woman. You can do it my girl!"

And that's what Penny did.

O.K. It wasn't easy keeping up the charade. In fact, it was the most difficult and demoralizing thing she'd ever done in her life, but when she saw the relief in Michael's eyes as his mouth voiced half-hearted protestations, she knew she'd done the right thing.

At least I had the courage to do the thing you should've done, she thought with disgust. *I'll never trust a man again. They aren't worth it.*

Telling Jane was just as hard and it took every ounce of Penny's self control not to blow the whole pretence and tell her so called friend exactly what she thought of her.

Would she ever get over that look of disbelief and disappointment on her parents face when she told them the wedding was off? It had been a dream come true for her mother to have her daughter marry a doctor. How close she came to blurting out the truth to her horrified parent, who, in her disappointment, had almost accused Penny of wrecking her life. But seeing the glint in her daughter's eyes, refrained from adding coals to the fire, so to speak.

Finally, everything was sorted; wedding preparations cancelled, friends and family informed. The deed was done.

And now what do I do, thought Penny, as once again she sought refuge in the Garden of Rest.

I can't carry on working at the hospital. It's too painful seeing Michael everyday and watching him and Jane together. I see the way they look at each other when they think no one is watching. It's time I left so they can get on with their lives and I can get on with mine, but where shall I go? I've only ever known Colhaven. I was born here, in this very hospital.

Penny needn't have worried. The solution was ready to knock her off her feet, literally.

CHAPTER TWO

The nurse staggered out of the ward carrying a pile of files earmarked for the filing office. Normally, Dave, the filing clerk would be collecting them, but as he was off sick today, Penny had volunteered to take them two flights down to the basement and hand them in, an offer she was now regretting.

Negotiating the corner leading to the lift, she turned her head and smiled at Mrs. Otis, who was being wheeled back to the ward in a wheelchair by her husband, and promptly crashed into a brick wall wearing a white coat, walking in the opposite direction.

Files flew everywhere and Penny landed on her back with a loud thud, knocking the breath out of her.

A bronzed arm and hand reached out, accompanied by a deep, masculine voice exclaiming, "I'm so very sorry. Are you all right? Are you hurt? No, don't move. Let's make sure no damage has been done."

Penny looked up into the suntanned face of a tall, well built man in his early thirties, his deep blue eyes showing concern as he swiftly and professionally examined the nurse, before declaring no obvious injuries. After insisting she sat for a few minutes to get her equilibrium, he then helped her to a standing position, and continued to apologise as he collected the scattered files.

"I'm fine, really I am," said Penny. "It was my fault. I wasn't looking where I was going. No, really, I haven't hurt anything. Just my pride a little."

That seems to be happening a lot lately, she thought ruefully.

She stopped talking as the human mountain towered over her, even though she was 5ft 8ins in her stocking feet.

"I'm Chris Maynard, a visiting doctor. And you are?"

"Penny Whickam. I'm a nurse at the hospital."

"Pleased to meet you, Penny," and the doctor held out his right hand in greeting. Hers disappeared in a strong, firm clasp.

"Please let me buy you a coffee in the cafeteria as an apology for literally knocking you off your feet. Where were you taking these files?"

"Down to the basement."

"Right. I'll escort you to make sure nothing else happens and then we'll have that coffee, O.K?"

He smiled at her, a lovely warm smile, reaching his eyes and showing dazzling white teeth, accentuated by his bronze face and sun bleached hair.

So, this is what a Greek god looks like, thought Penny, as she replied, "Well, I was going for my break after delivering these, so, thank you Doctor Maynard, I will accept your offer," and smiled back at him.

Ten minutes later, they were sitting at one of the tables in the hospital cafeteria, sipping cappuccinos whilst Penny listened intently to her companion.

"So, we really do need trained help. Leprosy is a forgotten disease. People have heard about it if they read the Bible, but not many know that it's still rife in Africa as well as India. Yes, it can be treated, but, like many illnesses, the sooner the treatment starts, the better. If it's left too long, the physical deformities it leaves are quite horrendous."

Penny was intrigued.

Doctor Chris Maynard had been living in Uganda, a country near the equator on the African continent, for the last two years. He was part of an international team of medical experts who visited developing countries helping to set up clinics and rehabilitation centres, or whatever that country needed in a medical sense, but didn't have the funds to do.

"This particular leprosy colony is actually run by Roman Catholic nuns. They are amazing, always smiling and cheerful. The colony miraculously survived during the time of Idi Amin, the dictator, who actually stopped all funding for the medication needed to treat the disease. It's a long-term illness, like tuberculosis. The treatment has to be taken every day for a minimum of six months, and it's not just one medication, but rather a cocktail of drugs, so it's relatively expensive. The nuns' work was totally funded by contributions from Ireland during that time. It's incredible they were able to maintain as well as they did. But they really needed help, and when Mother Superior heard about our work, she contacted us to see if we could help them both financially and with medical know-how. The buildings needed refurbishing, the clinic updating, and of course, along with leprosy, H.I.V. and A.I.D.S has been rearing its ugly head."

Chris paused, his mind thousands of miles away in deepest Africa.

"So, why have you come back to England?" asked Penny. "Are you on some kind of fundraiser or something?"

"Not fund raising as such, no. What I am looking for are medical personnel who would be willing to put their lives on hold for a year and come to Africa to help out in one or two places including The Haven, the leprosy colony I mentioned in Uganda. We have projects scattered throughout the continent, and need staff to help run them and at the same time teach the local population to do the same so that eventually we can leave them in the capable hands of indigenous experts. I know the director of Colhaven Hospital well. We actually trained together. I contacted him and received an invite to give a couple of lectures about the work we do in the hope of maybe getting a few personnel interested in joining us."

The doctor looked at Penny intently.

"Do you think there's a chance you'll come to the lectures?"

Penny's heart quickened.

Could this be the answer to her prayers? Maybe it was a kind of running away, but what a worthwhile thing to do, and in a country that held a certain fascination for her, ever since geography lessons at school.

"You know, Doctor Maynard, I could be interested in this type of work. That is if I'm suitably qualified. What qualifications are needed?"

Chris Maynard was silent for a moment.

He was strangely taken by this lovely young nurse who had an aura of sadness about her that she didn't voice but was only apparent when looking into those incredible violet- blue eyes. There was evidence of anguish and distress well hidden from the outside world, but not from the doctor.

"State registration for nurses, and we do recommend a course in tropical diseases for which we give the training. It's condensed into a month. Then of course, there are various immunisations you would need such as cholera, typhoid, yellow fever etc that we also organise."

The doctor paused in his narration.

"Are you sure you're serious? You haven't got carried away by the moment have you, Penny? It's a big decision, and certainly not for everybody. There are times when roughing it comes into the equation."

He hesitated for a second, and then asked the question that for some reason had been uppermost in his mind since literally bumping into this young woman. "Surely you have someone who wouldn't be so keen on seeing you go thousands of miles away from him?"

"I'm foot loose and fancy free, Doctor Maynard. It's important I find a new direction for my life, and this is the opportunity I believe I've been waiting for. The two of us colliding in the corridor was fate."

Fate it certainly was, thought the doctor, after he'd escorted Penny back to her ward. *She seems really keen on knowing more about the work we do. I hope to goodness she means it, as I certainly want to see her again. There's something very special about that young lady. She has an air of gentleness about her, which her patients must love. But, I'm convinced someone has hurt her very badly.*

The doctor walked to his car and drove the short distance to the hotel where he was staying for the duration of his visit.

Penny continued to occupy his thoughts as he received his key from reception and went to his room.

I wonder what mum and dad would think of her, and then laughed out loud at the thought. *Come on, Chris. You've only just met the girl. You didn't even ask her out which you can't do anyway, as technically, you'll be her boss if she decides to join the team, plus the fact she might say no.*

That thought alarmed him.

No, enough now. This must be strictly business. Relationships in the work place are bad news.

The doctor showered before changing for dinner. Looking at himself in the mirror he grinned ruefully and said, "Who are you trying to kid? You very much want to see her again. Goodness! Anyone would think you were seventeen," and he forced Penny from his mind whilst concentrating on trying not to cut himself shaving.

Chris Maynard came from a long line of doctors, and it seemed natural he would follow in the footsteps of his mother and father. However, he had an adventurous streak in him, and after doing mandatory stints at various hospitals in England, his quest for adventure and travel, along with using his practical skills as a doctor found a perfect bed fellow with the current organisation he was involved with. Yes, he'd had a few romantic attachments along the way, but nothing serious. His work was his passion. That is, until now.

Whilst sitting in solitary state in the hotel dining room, he found himself wishing Penny were his dining partner. Having coffee with the nurse had fed his desire for more of her company.

I so hope she comes to Africa. I would love to get to know her better, and then was stunned at the intensity of feelings the thought generated.

CHAPTER THREE

If Penny had foreseen the amount of opposition coming her way, she might well have had second thoughts about the whole thing.

Her mother was the main spokesman.

"But Penny, dear Penny, you can't possibly be serious! How can you even think of going to Africa of all places? Not now. I still don't understand why you broke off your engagement so suddenly to Michael, and now, not even two weeks later, you are planning to travel thousands of miles away to look after lepers! Are you depressed, Penny? Is that the reason you're doing this? Maybe you need a break, say a two-week holiday somewhere, but Africa for a year? No, Penny, this isn't right. Besides, you're not getting any younger. At twenty four you should be married and at least expecting your first baby, and my first grandchild!"

"Oh mother! That's enough. I need a change. I need to get away for a while, but I don't want a holiday. I want to do something with my life that will make a difference, and this will. At least read the literature Doctor Maynard gave me. It will give you a far better idea what it's all about. I really want yours and father's blessing for this new chapter in my life."

Michael and Jane were almost as bad.

By the time Penny told them what she'd planned to do, they knew that she knew they were a couple, however much they tried to cover it up. They both blamed themselves for chasing her away and so the recriminations continued until Penny felt like screaming with frustration.

What a relief when tropical disease training was completed, inoculations received, bags packed, passport renewed, farewells said, and finally she was in a mini bus travelling up the M1 to Heathrow Airport.

Penny had five other companions, all nurses, travelling in the bus. She turned to her next-door neighbour, smiled and said, "Hi, my name's Penny, Penny Whickam"

"Pleased to meet you, Penny. I'm Clair Dansbury, and that's Fiona Sutton sitting by that window, and next to her is Sally Field. We all trained together. I haven't been introduced to the other two."

"Tammy and Pammy Metcalf," a voice piped up. "Don't laugh. Our names are the bane of our lives, but mum and dad thought it was cute, cos we're twins," and two identical faces, sprinkled with freckles and sporting huge grins smiled at the other girls.

The ice was well and truly broken.

By the time Heathrow came into view, the six felt as though they'd known each other for years, and were chatting away like old friends.

Fiona and Sally were destined for an A.I.D.S clinic in Lesotho, whilst the twins were travelling further north up the continent to help out in a general hospital in Botswana. Clair and Penny had the prospect of working at the Haven leprosy colony situated near the town of Jinja in Uganda.

"I'm really glad we'll be together," said Clair. "I was just a little worried at the thought of being on my own in darkest Africa, knowing absolutely nobody. The idea was a bit daunting."

"Oh, so am I," said Penny. "Heaven knows what we're letting ourselves in for, but hearing the way Doctor Maynard describe the nuns at the colony, I'm sure we'll be fine. They sound absolutely delightful and totally dedicated. We'll learn so much from them."

Doctor Maynard was waiting for the nurses at the airport, his heart beating faster than usual in anticipation of seeing Penny again. Being in contact with her on almost a daily basis these past weeks, and having to act utterly professionally, had tested his self -control to the limit, and the thought she might change her mind at the last moment, and decide not to travel to Africa had been almost unbearable.

Seeing her chatting with the other nurses brought a huge sense of relief to the doctor, and he was able to greet them with enthusiasm.

"Nice to see you all again, ladies. Are you ready for your great African adventure? No second thoughts? If you have any, you'd better speak now because once we are on the plane, there will be no turning back."

"I believe I can speak for all of us when I say we're really looking forward to what lies ahead, Doctor Maynard. Am I right everyone?" asked Clair.

"Absolutely," the nurses chorused.

"That's great. I'm sure you won't regret your decision to take a year out of your careers to sample life African style. It'll be like nothing you've ever experienced before."

Doctor Maynard's enthusiasm was catching, and chattering like magpies, the girls saw their luggage disappear, passports stamped, boarding cards issued and they were ready to board the plane taking them to Johannesburg, South Africa. On arrival they would then go their separate ways to their various destinations.

Once settled on the plane, Penny felt herself really relax for the first time since she'd witnessed Michael and Jane together in the treatment room.

It had been so difficult pretending the decision to cancel the wedding was all her own doing. *Will I ever stop loving Michael?* she wondered. *How I wish one could turn love on and off like a tap. Even though I know I did the right thing, my heart makes me out to be a liar.*

She gave herself a mental shake.

No more looking back to the past. I can't change what has happened. Let me concentrate on the future. Who knows what adventures lie in store. As long as they don't include men I'll be fine.

"What do you think of our doctor, Penny?"

"Uh, I'm sorry Clair. What did you say? I was far away then."

Clair chuckled. "Doctor Maynard! What do you think of him? He's rather attractive, I'd say."

"Yes, I guess so. I haven't really given it much thought. He seems a very nice man. Obviously dedicated in what he does."

"Well, he's the type of person I could really go for. Do you know if he's married? I haven't noticed a wedding ring, and he hasn't mentioned a wife or family at all."

"He's never mentioned a wife or family in any conversation we've had. But I don't know if it's a good idea to get involved with someone if you're working with him or her professionally." *And I can certainly speak from experience on that topic,* she thought, before adding, "Anyway, is he coming to Uganda with us? He might be stopping off with the others in Lesotho or Botswana."

"Oh, he's coming to Uganda all right. He was telling me about plans to build an extension to the clinic."

Clair was silent for a while, her straight raven black hair framing her face like curtains, whilst her green eyes glistened as she contemplated the delectable doctor in her minds eye, her predatory instincts rising to the fore. From the very first moment Clair laid eyes on Chris Maynard she wanted him, and come hell or high water, she was going to have him, and woe betide anyone or anything that got in her way.

"I really do like him, Penny. You haven't got any feelings on the matter have you? You wouldn't be upset if I, well, pursued the subject, would you?"

"Of course not. Anyway, I'm off men period. I don't think I'll ever be able to trust a man again. He's all yours if you can get him."

"You sound as if you've had a bad experience, Penny. Do you want to talk about it?"

"No, not really. Suffice to say the old proverb of once bitten twice shy is one I'm going to be following from now on. I just want to enjoy my year in Uganda without relationships complicating things. They cause too much heartbreak. Personally, I don't believe they're worth it," and Penny turned her face away to look out of the window, not wanting Clair to see the tears welling up in her eyes at the thought of Michael and Jane together. How raw the wounds felt.

Damn it, will I ever get over him," thought Penny. *But I must. I'll make sure I'm so busy neither Michael or Jane will be able to sneak their way into my thoughts. Surely then the memories will fade.*

She sighed and turned back to Clair who was looking at her with a concerned expression on her face.

"Don't worry Clair. I'm fine. Just a bit tired after all the excitement of the last few weeks. I do believe the plane is moving. We'll be taking off soon."

Penny reached out her hand and gave Clair's a squeeze. "Uganda, here we come!"

The flight took eleven hours.

Penny slept fitfully, dozing rather than actually sleeping. She was relieved when she noticed the stewardesses moving around. Breakfast was being served.

Shouldn't be too long now before we reach Johannesburg. I won't be sorry to get off this plane and stretch my legs, she thought, and smiled at the stewardess handing her a tray.

"Wake up, Clair. Breakfast is ready and waiting, and I must say, it looks pretty appetizing; omelette, sausage, mushrooms and croissants. Plus a strong cup of coffee to blow the cobwebs away."

"Morning Penny," mumbled Clair. "Goodness, I'll be glad to land and sleep in a normal bed. I can never sleep well on a plane, ever. I always feel like death when I wake up. Where's that coffee you're bragging about?"

Penny grinned to herself. Clair was definitely not a daybreak person.

"Good morning ladies. Did you both manage to get a little sleep? Not easy, I know." Chris Maynard was towering over them. Penny noticed with some amusement how quickly Clair straightened herself in her seat and smiled sweetly at the doctor.

"The journey was perfect, Doctor Maynard," she answered. "Do you know how much longer it will be before we land at Johannesburg?"

"Less than an hour, Clair, and please call me Chris. You too, Penny. We are more colleagues in this venture, rather than boss and employee."

The doctor knew this wasn't strictly true, but determined to get to know Penny better once she was settled, he thought a hint in that direction wouldn't go amiss. Clair picked up on the suggestion straight away, and believing he was directing these words at her, responded immediately by saying, "Chris it is then."

With excitement mounting by the minute, Penny gathered her belongings together and soon the captain broadcast the temperature in Johannesburg was a pleasant 25C, and please fasten seat belts, as landing time was in twenty minutes.

Penny looked out of the window, amazed to see huge numbers of swimming pools dotting the landscape, plus sweeping expanses of sand from the gold mines the city was famous for, and then they were rolling along the tarmac of Johannesburg International Airport.

It was a different world, the sky a brilliant blue and shadows clear- cut, not hazy as in England, although the airport was very cosmopolitan as in other countries. A babble of languages could be heard, English being one of them, but also another language that was quite predominant, sounding guttural like German but actually quite different.

Penny asked Chris about it.

"You're hearing Afrikaans. It's similar to Dutch having its roots in seventeenth century Holland. The Dutch East Indies Company chose the Cape of Good Hope on the coast of South Africa for replenishing ships and as a resting place en route to the Indies in 1652. They brought the language with them; although over the years there've been subtle changes occurring. There are actually eleven official languages in South Africa due to the many different ethnic groups making up the population, which can be confusing. It's quite a melting pot."

Enthralled by it all, Penny stood silent, soaking up the atmosphere. Although most people were dressed in western clothes, here and there brightly coloured traditional costumes adorned a number of travellers, looking somewhat incongruous amidst the modern facilities.

"Right everyone, gather round," called Chris, and the nurses clustered about him as he went through their itinerary.

"Fiona and Sally, this is where we say goodbye. Once you've gone through passport control and claimed your luggage, you'll find a doctor waiting for you at arrivals. He'll be holding a board with your names written on it. His name is Günter, and he's a German doctor working at the clinic in Lesotho, and a very good friend of mine. He offered to drive you to Lesotho, which I'm sure you'll enjoy, as the scenery is magnificent, very mountainous. I've just spoken to Günter on my mobile, and he's there looking out for you. Have a great time, and I'll see you during the course of the year. You have my mobile number if you need to get in touch with me."

There were hugs all round, then Fiona and Sally disappeared amongst all the other passengers making their way to passport control.

Penny said goodbye with mixed feelings. Although she'd only known them for a short time, she'd felt they were all in this adventure together, forgetting for a while the party would split once they reached Africa.

The twins will soon get their plane to Botswana, so that will just leave Chris, Clair and myself, she thought.

The doctor spoke again, bringing Penny out of her reverie.

"Tammy and Pammy, you'll get the connecting flight to Botswana which leaves in 45 minutes, so just go through that door to the internal flight departure lounge where you'll meet another friend of mine, Gert, whose also a doctor working at the hospital in Botswana. He's Afrikaans, but his English is excellent, so you won't have any problems in understanding him. He's been on holiday at the Kruger National Park, and offered to travel with you so you wouldn't get lost and end up in Zambia or Malawi or wherever."

"Well, that's a relief," said the twins in unison.

Laughter broke out amongst the group that had gone unusually quiet. Tensions eased and goodbyes were said.

"So," continued the doctor, "that leaves just the two of you. Don't look so apprehensive, Clair. I'll be with you all the way to Uganda. In fact, you won't be getting rid of me for a while as I promised Sister Magdalene when I returned, I would supervise the construction of a new wing being added to the clinic. Remember I told you about it. When you meet Sister Magdalene, you'll understand why I wouldn't dream of not doing what she asks."

"Goodness, she sounds like a termagant," said Clair, her green eyes gleaming as she smiled coquettishly at the doctor.

Chris laughed. "Not quite that actually. She's five foot nothing and has the face of a saint, but her backbone is made of steel, and when it comes to her beloved patients, nothing is too good for them. She'll fight tooth and nail to get the things they need. She must be eighty easily, but is incredibly sprightly and, if rumour is correct, actually had a set too with Idi Amin himself when he was dictator, and apparently sent him packing. She fears nothing and nobody."

Clair smiled at the doctor. "Well, I hope she doesn't send me packing. I'll work hard to make sure I stay in her good books."

"As long as you have the interest of the colony at heart, she'll be like a mother hen clucking over you. Now, our connecting flight is in just over an hour. So, how would you both like a coffee before we get our boarding passes?"

"That sounds fine by me," said Clair. "How about you, Penny? Fancy a coffee before we start the final leg of our journey?"

"Yes, I would. My mouth's quite dry. Excitement I expect," and Penny smiled at the two of them, her magnificent eyes sparkling in anticipation of what was lying ahead of her.

Doctor Chris Maynard was captivated, and knew it. The idea of love at first sight had always seemed fanciful to him until he first looked deeply into Penny's eyes over coffee at the hospital. Remembering that moment, he knew he'd fallen in love there and then and realised she was the person he'd always hoped to meet but never thought he would.

Whoever had caused the aura of sadness he'd seen deep within her was an idiot, as far as he was concerned. "Well, his loss, my gain," thought Chris, who had no doubt a man was responsible for the barrier Penny had subconsciously put up. "It won't be easy gaining my darling's trust," he surmised, as he ushered the two nurses through the door of the restaurant in the departures lounge. It was only then he realised Clair had been talking to him.

"I'm sorry Clair. What were you saying?"

"I said how nice it will be working with you," she replied, a little affronted he hadn't been paying her any attention. "I expect you'll be showing us the ropes, so to speak, I hope?" and she looked at the doctor keenly.

"Well, I shall be around of course, but you'll be working with the nuns who are all trained nurses in their own right." He turned his attention to Penny, who was sitting quietly at the table, drinking her coffee which the waiter had delivered, along with a plate of koeksisters, a South African delicacy of sweet dough covered in ice cold syrup.

"You're very quiet, Penny. I hope you aren't having second thoughts?"

"Oh, no. Absolutely not. Although I know I'm sitting here in South Africa, it almost feels like a dream, and soon I'll wake up in my flat at Colhaven."

"It's no dream, Penny. And in a little while the realities of living in Africa will hit you, and then you may wish it really had been a dream, but I hope not," and he looked deep into those beautiful eyes and wished he really knew what she was thinking and feeling.

Clair saw the look Doctor Maynard gave Penny, and her stomach churned with resentment.

I wish he'd stare at me like that. Penny isn't even aware of the way he's looking at her. Still, that's not a bad thing. That gives me time to go to work on the doctor myself whilst she continues to nurse her broken heart. Long may it stay broken, and she smiled to herself. *Alls fair in love and war,* and turned her attention to the doctor, keeping him occupied until boarding the plane for Entebbe airport in Uganda.

They arrived during a torrential downpour.

"Get used to this, girls," laughed Chris, as they scurried across the tarmac to the airport buildings. "This is the rainy season. However, Mother Nature does give a warning before she dumps tons of water on you. Ten minutes before the rain starts, a wind begins to blow, and you know you have only that ten minutes to get under cover before the heavens open."

By the time they reached the airport terminal, they were soaked to the skin.

Clair looked like a bedraggled rat, her black hair hanging in tails, but Penny's chestnut curls, although rain – soaked, framed her heart shaped face, accentuating high cheekbones and full lips. With eyes sparkling like wine, and perfect teeth showing in a wide grin, Doctor Maynard thought she had never looked so desirable. Her wet clothes clung to a body that definitely had all the curves in the right places, giving the doctor an almighty struggle to put his imagination on hold, and remain business like, no easy task.

"Right," he said brusquely, "a land rover is waiting for us outside the airport. It won't take long to get our luggage and then we'll drive pass Jinja and on to The Haven. Your clothes will dry by the time we reach our destination, unless you want to change first?" Both girls shook their heads. "The rain comes down in short, sharp bursts, and then the next thing you know, everything is steaming in the heat. It's like living in a sauna at times."

Clair manoeuvred herself quickly to the seat next to the doctor, much to his frustration, leaving Penny no option but to sit at the back.

The nurse didn't mind. She was content looking out of the window, fascinated by mud huts with thatched roofs built in clusters around small courtyards where chickens roamed freely, pecking at what ever was available to eat. She waved back at youngsters wearing the minimum of clothing in the muggy heat, as they ran through rain puddles, behaving like kids the world over. They drove through banana and coffee plantations, stopping once to let a troop of monkeys cross the road. Penny noticed mist rising from the thick vegetation as the sun poured out its heat now that the rain had stopped.

"Chris is right. Uganda could be described as one big sauna," convinced she could see steam rising off her clothes.

After driving for nearly two hours, the last bit on a dirt track through bush, they came upon a cluster of white, one-storey buildings, built in a semicircle, all facing a circular courtyard. In the centre was a splendid white marble fountain, with a green marble dolphin spouting water out of its upturned snout. They had arrived at The Haven, home for the next year.

Penny clambered out of the land rover and stood admiring the fountain.

"Yes, I know it looks absurd, stuck in the middle of the bush," remarked Chris, "but a benefactor thought it would look nice. Anyway, the kids love playing in the water, and talk of the devil, here they come now."

"Uncle Chris, uncle Chris, you come back, you come back!"

A chorus of voices heralded the arrival of half a dozen children, ages ranging from about three up to ten who flung themselves upon "Uncle Chris."

He laughingly grabbed the nearest child and swung him around off the ground, much to the delight of the rest, who shouted, "Me! Me!" in unison.

"Later, children," said Doctor Maynard. "First let me introduce you to the new nurses who will be working here for a year. This is Clair and this is Penny."

The girls said hullo, and a chorus of hellos bellowed back at them. Penny was enchanted.

How friendly they are, she thought. *I wonder if they're the children of patients who have leprosy? They certainly don't appear sick.*

"Take their bags, children, and carry them to the nurses' rooms."

The doctor turned to Penny and Clair. "I want to introduce you to Mother Superior and then take you to your quarters. I'm sure you would like a shower and freshen up before lunch. Then I'll show you around The Haven. I hope you're hungry. I could eat a horse. Ah, there's Sister Magdalene coming out of the clinic," and Doctor Maynard hurried to where a tiny lady in a white habit, using a walking stick, was carefully negotiating the path that led from the clinic to the courtyard.

The two nurses waited quietly whilst the doctor escorted the nun to where they were standing.

"Penny, Clair. This is Sister Magdalene, Mother Superior of The Haven, of whom I am absolutely terrified, and if you're sensible, you'll be terrified of her too. Sister Magdalene, this is Penny," and he gestured towards Penny, "and this is Clair."

"I am so pleased to meet you both," said Mother Superior, and held out her arms to give each girl a hug. "Take no notice of what the doctor is saying. Terrified of me indeed! And I'm so tiny compared to this giant." and she gave Doctor Maynard a playful tap on the leg with her walking stick.

"I'm very happy you both decided to come and help us here at The Haven. I so hope your stay will be enjoyable and that you will consider your time spent with us worthwhile. Now, I'm sure you would like to freshen up before lunch, so Doctor Maynard will show you to your rooms and I shall meet you in the dining room say, in an hour. Will that be convenient for you?"

"Sounds perfect, Sister Magdalene," said Clair.

"Good. Off you go and I'll see you later."

The girls followed the doctor to the staff quarters.

Penny was pleasantly surprised. They each had a small room, painted in a soft apricot colour with matching curtains. The furnishings consisted of a bed, chest of drawers and wardrobe, all painted white, plus a small oak desk and chair complete with writing paper and airmail envelopes, which Penny thought was a nice touch. Mosquito netting surrounded the bed whose crisp white sheets and pillowcases looked very inviting. A ceiling fan spun lazily creating a gentle breeze as soft as feathers on Penny's skin. A tiny lizard raced over the ceiling and down a wall to disappear behind the chest of drawers. Penny found out later it was a gecko, totally harmless and very cute.

The nurse looked longingly at the bed, realising she felt exhausted, not just from the journey, but also from the emotional roller coaster she'd been on these last couple of months.

Well, a refreshing shower and something to eat will perk me up, I'm sure, and went next door to Clair's room to find her partner already heading towards the bathroom.

"I won't be long, Penny. I'll knock when I've finished."

"No problem, Clair. I'll make a start with unpacking."

That didn't take long. The girls were provided with white tops and slacks as uniforms, and advised to pack summer clothes, as Uganda was hot! By the time Penny hung her last dress in the wardrobe, Clair was knocking on the door, calling all clear.

Within the hour, both girls were making their way to the dining room with Chris, whose heart melted when he saw Penny in a buttercup yellow blouse and slacks, showing off her slim figure to perfection, as well as accentuating the chestnut hues in her thick curly hair falling to her shoulders

The amazing thing is, thought the doctor, *Penny is totally oblivious to her beauty. She's as beautiful on the inside as she is on the outside. Chris, my boy, I do believe you've got it bad. I have never felt like this about anyone before,* and gave a rueful grin before saying; "I'll take you for a guided tour after we've eaten. Sister Magdalene is a stickler for time keeping," he added, whilst opening a door in the complex to reveal a large, airy dining room with a dozen round tables each able to seat six persons.

Three tables were occupied; one with chattering nuns, all wearing white habits, one with other staff from the colony including the gardener and handyman, and at the third table sat Sister Magdalene with her second in command on her right.

"Oh, good, here you are. Please sit with me, and Martha and Naomi will bring you your lunch."

Penny was to find out later that nearly all the children and adults had Biblical names they were known by as well as their tribal ones, a reminder of the days when Christian missionaries had braved the rigours of Africa to bring the Gospel to the so called heathens.

"Now," said Sister Magdalene, "I would like to introduce you to Sister Mary. She is my right hand man so to speak and I rely on her for the smooth running of The Haven."

Sister Mary looked to be in her sixties, a tall, thin lady whose formidable exterior hid a true softie inside. Penny found out later the patients and children absolutely adored her.

She smiled a welcome at the nurses, and waved her hand towards two chairs opposite her and Mother Superior.

"I'm very pleased to meet you both. We're losing two of our nuns who are going back to Ireland on furlough for a year. In fact, they have already left, so you'll be plunging in at the deep end, taking their places. However, we shall all make you feel very welcomed, and please, don't hesitate to ask any questions you may have. We really are one big happy family here, but of course, our main concern is for the welfare of the patients and their families."

...Ten o'clock that night, Penny lay flat on her back in bed, hands tucked underneath her head looking up at the mosquito netting, reflecting on a day that had passed like a whirlwind.

Introductions were made to the other staff.

Penny particularly remembered Moses, the gardener. (She privately thought at the time Methuselah might have been a more appropriate name, as he looked so old). He had had leprosy, which was now cured, but the resulting deformities had caused him to lose several digits off both hands and feet, but he was able to wield a trowel with gusto and kept the grounds immaculate, as well as cultivating all the fresh produce The Haven needed. His pride and joy was a huge cascading bush of bougainvillea guarding the entrance to Mother Superior's office. He absolutely adored the nun. The colours of red, yellow, orange and violet were intermixed, creating the illusion of the plant bursting into flames when the sun played on it. *No, I think Moses is definitely the right name for this gentleman*, thought Penny, remembering the story she'd heard as a child in Sunday school, about Moses and the burning bush.

After a delicious lunch of cold meats and salad with freshly cut paw-paw, Doctor Maynard showed Penny and Clair around the compound, introducing them to the nuns and patients in the three wards they had for men, women and children. There were about fifteen patients in each. Then he showed them the recreation room where patients well enough could socialise to gossip and do arts and crafts such as bead-work and wood sculptor, which was sent to Jinja and even Kampala, the capital of Uganda, to sell to the burgeoning tourist trade for much needed funds.

Then it was time for the evening meal, consisting of various cuts of meat, barbecued on racks resting on oil drums cut in half, length ways, and eaten with salad and a thick maize meal porridge with a delicious tomato gravy.

Whilst eating, a dozen young girls serenaded the group, singing and humming the timeless songs of Africa, a throbbing beat causing them to sway in unison, grass skirts rustling, caught up in the magic that is the Dark Continent.

Now I really know I'm thousands of miles away from home, thought Penny, moving in time to the music, her eyes closed as she savoured the moment.

Doctor Maynard was transfixed.

The light from the fire cast shadows on Penny's face, emphasising her high cheekbones, the chestnut of her hair alive and glowing as the short twilight turned to darkness. His gaze rested on her full lips, and a longing, almost painful in its intensity, descended upon him, demanding that he taste the delights of her desirable mouth.

This will not do, Chris thought, and tore his gaze away from Penny, only to encounter the searching eyes of Clair.

She was devastated.

Why doesn't Chris look at me like that? Penny is totally unaware of him. It just isn't fair. I know I'm not unattractive. How can I get him interested in me?

She sat brooding, her natural vindictive nature, usually kept well hidden, now coming to the fore, scattering seeds of jealousy deep within her, festering and multiplying as various ideas came to mind. She discarded them all until a tiny piece of a plan began to form, just a glimmer of an idea she knew she would have to think carefully about before putting into action. It was obvious Penny was her rival regardless whether the other nurse knew it or not. And Clair was not used to having rivals. She didn't like the fact one bit.

The evening drew to an end.

Penny was having great difficulty in keeping her eyes open.

She leant towards Clair and said, "If I don't go to bed now, I'll never get up in the morning. I'm saying goodnight, and how glad I am to be sharing this experience with you, (which made Clair feel a momentary pang of guilt that went as quickly as it came) and I shall see you in the morning. What time did Sister Mary say for us to meet in the staff office? Oh yes, seven – thirty. I'll see you for breakfast at seven then. Good night Sister Magdalene and Sister Mary. Thank you for the lovely welcome you've given us. Good night Chris. I'll see you in the morning."

Doctor Maynard scrambled to his feet. "Can I escort you to your room, Penny?" he asked hopefully.

"No thank you. I'm sure that won't be necessary. You stay and enjoy yourself," and to his chagrin, Penny disappeared into the night.

If Clair thought she would now be able to make some headway with the doctor, she was doomed to disappointment, because within minutes of the nurse's departure, Chris decided to turn in as well.

Penny, totally unaware of these overtones, smiled to herself as she pulled open the mosquito netting and looked out at the myriads of stars through her bedroom window.

I didn't think of Michael or Jane once during this magical evening. That bodes well for the future, and with that comforting thought, pulled the netting shut and drifted off into a dreamless sleep, only to be woken by a cock crowing as dawn broke over the African bush the following morning.

CHAPTER FOUR

Penny stretched luxuriously.

What a lovely sleep. I haven't slept like that for weeks.

She looked around at the unfamiliar surroundings, memories flooding her mind of the unforgettable day and evening she'd so enjoyed.

Well, Penny Whickam, you really are in Uganda, in the middle of Africa, and The Haven is your home for the next year, so, let's see what today has to offer," and jumped out of bed to have a quick shower before donning her uniform as a fully fledged member of staff.

She met Clair in the dining room.

"Good morning Clair," said Penny. "What a lovely day it is. Did you sleep well?"

"Morning," answered Clair grumpily. "Not really. All I could hear were millions of crickets making a racket all night. How you can look so bright and breezy at," Clair looked at her watch "seven in the morning, I'll never know."

Penny just smiled, remembering how moody the nurse was on the flight, knowing she was not a morning person, and prepared to make allowances. How fortunate the time of day didn't affect her naturally sunny disposition.

"Penny," said Clair, "I want to speak to you."

Clair stopped talking as the door to the dining room opened and Doctor Chris Maynard walked in.

"Good morning ladies," he said, his heart missing a beat as he spotted Penny helping herself to cereal. "I hope you both slept well?"

"Like a top," answered Clair. "I was saying to Penny the sound of crickets is really soothing, almost like a lullaby sending you to sleep."

Penny glanced at Clair in surprise but didn't say anything. She smiled her good morning to the doctor and carried on eating her cereal. It was obvious Clair would say anything to impress Chris. No problem. She'd had enough of men. All she wanted was do a good job and learn and experience as much as she could in the time she had here. Future plans were on hold.

Doctor Maynard outlined their itinerary, as Sister Mary was unavailable due to a family crisis with one of the patients.

"Clair, you'll be working on the men's ward for now, and Penny, you will be with the women. Those are the two vacancies made available with the nuns gong back to Ireland. You start at 7.30, finish at 12 midday for 2 hours, mainly because it's too hot to do anything, and then back on duty at 2 until 5, with two days off a week, sometimes together, sometimes not. How does that sound?"

"I believe we can manage that, eh Penny?" said Clair.

"Certainly better times than the split shift work and night duty I had to do at the hospital."

"Good. I'll leave you to report to your wards, and will see you later, probably at lunch," and Doctor Maynard breezed out of the door, determined to make an impromptu visit to the women's ward to see how Penny was getting on.

After all, he thought, *it's all new to her and she might be pleased to have me show her the ropes… Don't try and kid yourself, Chris. You just want to have an excuse to look into those beautiful eyes and smell that wonderful freshness she has about her.*

He shook his head. This was not good for his peace of mind.

Meanwhile, Penny, totally unaware of the turmoil her presence was causing Dr Maynard, hurried to the women's ward and reported to the nun in charge; her name, Sister Mercy.

"Welcome Nurse Whickam," smiled Sister Mercy, whose rotund face housed bright button eyes peeping out from under her habit. "I hope you enjoy your stay with us. I know Doctor Maynard introduced you to the patients yesterday, so I shall bring you up to date on their treatment and rehabilitation," and she bustled away at an alarming pace, her plump body no hindrance whatsoever to the swiftness of her tapping shoes. Penny struggled to keep up.

The morning passed quickly for the nurse.

Sister Mercy demonstrated different types of dressings used for patients who'd come too late to prevent physical deformities. She explained the times and dosages of medications used in the treatment and the general care given. Penny assisted patients in washing and dressing, as well as helping feed breakfast to those unable to do so themselves. One young woman named Ruth, who'd gone into labour two nights previous, particularly touched her heart. Her tiny baby daughter was beside her in bed, lying in a shoebox, snuggled up nice and warm in a cut up feather soft blanket. Penny helped change the baby and then positioned her on her mother's breast at feeding time, as Ruth's disabilities made this difficult for the young mother to do.

It was during this time Doctor Maynard came to the ward.

He stood for a minute watching Penny gently hold the baby as she suckled. She was quietly crooning to her, at the same time, smiling encouragingly at Ruth as the baby groped for her nipple.

"There," he heard Penny say, "See how strong she is. She is sucking very well. And you are doing very well too," and she smiled encouragement at the young mother. Ruth whispered thank you and looked down at her baby with such tender love, Penny felt a lump in her throat and tears came to her eyes.

"I see mother and child are bonding very well," and Penny glanced up to see Doctor Maynard looking at her with an odd expression on his face.

She blinked away tears threatening to overflow and smiled at the doctor. "Yes, they are doing well." Penny tucked a pillow under Ruth's arm to help support the baby, and quietly walked away from the bed when she was satisfied that mother and baby were comfortable. She glanced up at the doctor.

"I was wondering if Ruth will have prosthetic hands so she'd be able to look after her baby herself."

"That's in the pipeline. They are expensive and not always successful, but we shall obviously do what we can for her. Ruth's future depends on how she'll manage as a wife, which to these people is most important. Will she be able to cook, clean, look after her children, ground the corn and feed the chickens? Or will she become destitute? Hopefully, her husband to be will stand by her."

Doctor Maynard looked at Penny intently.

"She's proved she's fertile by producing a healthy baby, which often has to happen before a marriage will take place, but it isn't a full gone conclusion. Women's lib is also not a well-known concept in this country. Tribal traditions are powerful in Africa, and it takes a brave woman to go against them."

He smiled. "Anyway, that's enough serious talk for now, Nurse Whickam. Sister Mercy has told me you've fifteen minutes for a break, so, would you mind if I keep you company with a cool drink under the baobab tree?"

"It will be my pleasure, Doctor Maynard. I wonder if Clair is also free, then she could join us."

Chris Maynard inwardly groaned. Clair was the last person he wanted to have impinging on his time spent with Penny, but his love had spotted her friend in the distance as they settled themselves on the garden chairs placed around the tree, and was calling to her.

"Come and join us, Clair. We're having a drink break under the baobab."

"Coming" and Clair hurried over to where the two were sitting drinking glasses of freshly squeezed orange juice which Martha, one of the kitchen staff, had brought for them.

"One more, please Martha, for Nurse Clair," said Doctor Maynard, and proceeded to be polite by asking Clair how she was enjoying her first day on the male ward.

"I'm loving it. Sister Angelica is a honey and has taught me so much already. I'm amazed at how cheerful the patients are, considering the awful deformities most of them have been left with before the leprosy was treated. What an awful disease. I remember you saying at your lectures there are 10-12 million people affected by leprosy in the world, and yet so few people in the west really know anything about it."

"That's the problem," replied the doctor. "Most people affected either live in Africa or India. The incubation period is also prolonged ranging from 2-5 years, so getting treatment started at an early stage before the deformities set in is difficult. Detection is severely handicapped by the social stigma associated with leprosy. The World Health Organisation has estimated 50% of all leprosy cases are actually not reported. That's a scary thought."

Chris shook his head. "Another big problem we have is there's no vaccination as yet against the Mycobacterium Leprae which, as you know, is the bug that causes all the problems. However, there are trials that look promising using the B.C.G. vaccine against tuberculosis. There are places where the incidence of leprosy has dropped by as much as 80%, but in other places, only by 20%. So, there's a long way to go, but it's a start. Education is the key so the indigenous population can recognise the early symptoms of numbness in the extremities and come to the clinic before the bug gets hold."

Doctor Maynard smiled wryly at the two girls. "I'd better get off my soap box and let you two get back to work before I'm in trouble with the nuns. I'll see you later at lunch," and the doctor strode off towards the new building works that he was supervising for the extension to the clinic.

Clair looked longingly after him. "He is absolutely gorgeous. I'm amazed he hasn't already been snapped up."

She looked at Penny and decided to be blunt with her. "I asked some questions and our doctor isn't married, and doesn't even have a girlfriend. So, Penny, you wouldn't mind making yourself scarce so I can spend more time alone with him. I know I've a chance with Chris if he has time on his own to get to know me. What do you say?"

Penny looked at Clair with understanding in her eyes. "Of course I'll do anything I can to smooth the passage of true love, and if that means doing a disappearing act, so be it."

"Thanks. I really appreciate that. Now, it's back to the grindstone. I'll see you at lunch."

Penny walked back to her ward, waving at Clair before she disappeared through the doors.

The rest of the morning passed quickly, and once the patients had eaten their lunch, it was time to make her way to the dining room for her own meal.

As she opened the door, she saw Clair chatting away to Doctor Maynard. So, mindful of what her friend had requested earlier, Penny waved, and then sat at another table with a couple of nuns. Martha placed a plate of food in front of her, and she was about to eat when to her consternation, Doctor Maynard sat down next to her.

She quickly glanced at Clair, and then wished she hadn't.

Oh my goodness. If looks could kill, that's me dead, and with a sinking heart, she turned her head towards the doctor who was saying, "after you finish at five would you like to come to Jinja with me? I have to pick up supplies for the colony Sister Magdalene has organised."

"Thank you for asking, Chris, but if you don't mind, I think I'll spend my time writing letters. I know mother will be watching the postman like a hawk, so I wouldn't like to disappoint her. Another time maybe? Have you asked Clair? I'm sure she would really appreciate the trip."

No Penny. I haven't asked Clair. It's you I want to spend time with, not Clair, thought Doctor Maynard, but he just smiled and said, "No problem. I understand perfectly. When you've finished letter writing, let me have them and I'll make sure they are taken to Jinja for posting," and the doctor continued to make small talk whilst Penny finished her lunch.

After drinking a glass of orange juice, the nurse politely excused herself, in the hope Doctor Maynard would go back to Clair.

That didn't happen

Chris stayed sitting at the table for a few minutes, looking at the closed door Penny had walked through.

This is not going to be easy. Whoever has hurt Penny, hurt her badly. I'll have to tread very carefully otherwise I'll frighten her off. O.K. my darling, if that's what it takes to win your heart, I will be patience personified. Now that I've finally found the woman of my dreams, there's no way I'm going to lose her, regardless how long its going to take, and with that thought running through his mind, the doctor left the dining room to go back to his building project, before doing ward rounds.

Clair remained seated, her antagonism towards Penny rapidly turning to loathing. The fact that the nurse had done nothing to encourage Chris didn't come into the equation. She was Clair's rival and in her world, rivals were to be disposed of by any means possible. From now on, Penny Whickam was public enemy number one.

The afternoon passed quickly. Penny enjoyed working with Sister Mercy, who had a wicked sense of humour causing the nurse to double up with laughter at the exploits she recounted.

"Yes, Penny, it's all very well for you to laugh, but to be chased by an amorous old ostrich who desperately needed glasses is no joke. Fancy mistaking me for a potential mate just because I was wearing a black and white habit! Luckily Doctor Maynard attracted the ostrich's attention before I was flattened. Such a lovely man is our Doctor Maynard. How he hasn't been snapped up by now, I'll never know. We've had nurses galore here, and he never showed the slightest bit of interest in any of them, that is, until now," and she peeped at the nurse, her button eyes twinkling with merriment.

"Oh, do you really think he's interested in Clair? I sincerely hope so. She is totally taken with him," exclaimed Penny.

"Clair! No, I'm not talking about Clair. It's you he can't take his eyes off! If anyone has fallen hook, line and sinker, it's our Doctor Maynard for Nurse Penny Whickam."

The nurse looked mystified.

"No! You must be mistaken, Sister Mercy. Doctor Maynard isn't interested in me that way. He's just being friendly that's all. So, enough of your over romantic notions. I'm going to Ruth as its time for her to be feeding her baby," and Penny turned to escape the inquisitive stare of the nun, who had to have the last word.

"I'm never wrong in these things, Penny. You'll see, I'm never wrong."

Penny's mind was in turmoil as she gently helped Ruth suckle her baby.

What is Sister Mercy thinking of? Chris isn't interested in me like that. I'm sure he isn't. I don't need any more complications in my life. But is that why Clair looked daggers at me in the dining room? Has she noticed something I haven't? Penny wasn't convinced and when she next met Doctor Maynard, she knew she was right because he couldn't have been more businesslike if he'd tried.

Than goodness for that, thought Penny. *Sister Mercy is definitely barking up the wrong tree. You have nothing to fear from me, Clair. Go all out and get him.*

Penny didn't have an inkling of the superhuman effort it took for Chris Maynard to be professional. During their conversation about such mundane matters as a reminder not to forget to take her anti malarial tablets, the doctor's eyes were drawn to Penny's full, perfectly shaped lips, looking so ripe to be kissed.

Now, Chris, remember what you told yourself in the dining room. For you to win Penny's heart, take things nice and easy. She's like a gazelle that will disappear in an instance if startled. When you eventually do get that kiss, which you will, it will certainly be worth waiting for.

His fingers felt compelled to twine themselves around her chestnut curls and gently pull her towards him and have her in his arms, to drown himself in her beautiful eyes, knowing she was his forever, and woe betide anyone who tried to take her away from him.

He returned to earth with a bump.

"I'm sorry, Sister Mercy. What did you say?"

The nun smiled knowingly at the doctor.

"I said, Doctor Maynard, Penny can go off duty now. I know it's a little early, but we are up to date with everything, and shame, she has worked very hard, and her first day as well, in this heat. Off you go, my dear, and I'll see you in the morning," and Sister Mercy bustled away, but not before giving Penny a meaningful look, which the nurse totally ignored. After all, she knew better.

She walked with Chris to the entrance of the ward.

"Right, Penny. I'm off to do some paper work. Have a nice evening. I'll see you at breakfast," and Doctor Maynard strode off quickly before his resolve broke and he asked the nurse to accompany him for a stroll around the gardens.

If she was surprised by his abrupt departure, Penny didn't dwell on it. She decided to do a little exploring on her own before letter writing. All staff had been warned not to venture out of the compound, because of wild animals foraging in the bush, so she followed a meandering path around the back of the buildings.

Moses has really done a good job with the gardens, thought Penny, as she came to a large alcove surrounded on three sides by huge bougainvillea bushes, this time, resplendent in deep purple. A wooden bench beckoned from the middle of the alcove, calling out to Penny to sit and rest and just enjoy the luscious surroundings.

The nurse didn't hesitate.

She lowered herself onto the seat and leaning back, closed her eyes and savoured the smells and sounds of the African bush. Initially, there seemed to be silence, but the undercurrent buzzing of myriads of insects gave way to the different calls of swooping birds, eating on the wing, as the setting sun encouraged flying ants to leave their holes in the ground and venture forth. Now and again, Penny heard the barking of baboons calling out to each other, and she smiled, excitement rising, as she realised this was truly her home for the whole year.

I'm so glad I made the decision to come to Uganda. Michael and Jane seem so far away, not just in distance, but also as distant memories. Yes, this was the best thing I could've done, and she felt herself slipping away into a dreamless sleep… to be abruptly awoken by Doctor Maynard saying in a tense voice, "Keep still Penny! What ever you do, don't move!"

When Penny reached the alcove, she hadn't realised the building opposite housed the office of Chris Maynard.

He was sat at his desk, facing the window, papers in front of him, staring into space. Now and again, he picked up his pen to tick off the list of building materials he required from Jinja, only to place it back on the desk.

This is no good. I just can't concentrate. I'm looking at this list, but all I'm seeing is Penny's face. Come on, Chris! Enough is enough. You have a job to do, and acting like a love sick teenager will not get it done.

He moved away from the desk and walked to the window, only to feel his heart do a somersault when he saw Penny walk into the alcove and sit down on the wooden bench.

"That's torn it," he muttered, staring longingly at the woman of his dreams, her head flung back, chestnut curls cascading down to her shoulders, unrestricted from the pony tail she wore on duty. With slim legs stretched out in front of her, hands lightly clasped behind her head inadvertently causing the material of her tunic to tighten over and emphasise the fullness of her breasts, Penny had no concept of the desirable picture she made in the frame of the doctor's window.

How the hell am I going to concentrate now?

He paced backwards and forwards in front of the window, desperately resisting the urge to go out and join the nurse.

"No, I must let her have her space. She obviously has issues she needs to deal with. I'll only complicate matters," he muttered under his breath and took one last look at the sleeping Penny before going back to his desk.

Hold on, what's that? he thought and then to his horror, realised he'd seen the movement of a green mamba, one of the most poisonous snakes in Africa, slowly slithering its way closer and closer to the sleeping Penny.

Chris didn't hesitate.

He grabbed the snake catcher he always kept in his office, raced out of the door, and then carefully made his way into the alcove, the noose ready to trap the snake's head. As the doctor was about to pounce, Penny stirred in her sleep, causing the snake to rear up, ready to strike. Chris shouted, and at the same time, grabbed the snake around its neck, looping the noose over the head, pulling it tight.

Penny woke up startled.

She looked at the doctor, and then at the snake, then looked at the doctor again.

"You're safe now Penny," he said, and quickly killed the reptile with his knife before throwing its remains outside the compound.

Penny sat frozen, her heart racing wildly.

I would've died if Chris hadn't acted so quickly, she thought, and breathed deeply, trying to slow her heart- beat.

Chris sat down beside her, placing an arm around her shoulders, feeling her trembling.

"It's all right, Penny. Everything is fine now. There's nothing to worry about," he murmured, cradling her in his arms, mentally thanking the now demised snake for giving him the opportunity to put into action what he'd been wanting to do since he'd first set eyes on the nurse.

She laid her head against his broad shoulder, thus enabling him to feel her silky hair brushing against his cheek. He felt her trembling body slowly relax in his comforting embrace, her racing heart slowing to a steady beat.

Time stood still for the doctor. In his arms was the woman he absolutely adored with every ounce of his being. Her body melted into his embrace, a perfect union that was meant to be. *If I died now, I would die a very happy man*, thought the doctor, as he savoured the moment.

"Thank you, Chris. I'm fine now," and Penny stirred in his arms.

He immediately let go, albeit reluctantly.

But not before Clair saw them.

She'd been walking towards the dining room, when she spotted movement in the alcove. Curious as to what was happening, Clair tiptoed along the path and peeped around the bougainvillea bushes. What she thought she was witnessing filled her with fury. There was her arch-rival deliberately ensnaring her love.

The little cat! And after she'd told me she'd no interest in Chris whatsoever. Right Penny, you bitch! So that's your game is it? Well, you've met your match in me, and Clair crept away, the green eyed monster of jealousy rising up within her, taking absolute control of every aspect of her psyche.

CHAPTER FIVE

Days passed into weeks.

For Penny, it was an idyllic time.

She got on well with staff and patients alike, and felt blessed when Ruth told her the name she was known by amongst the Ugandans.

"In English it means, "as beautiful as a dove," which is how we feel about you. The dove is beautiful inside as well as outside. It is gentle and caring, just like you, Nurse Penny," and Ruth smiled shyly, as Penny handed over her now chubby baby.

Tears welled up into Penny's eyes.

How lovely to have them think of me like that, she thought, whilst helping Ruth position the baby to feed. *They are so grateful for everything that is done for them.*

"You look a thousand miles away."

Chris's deep, manly voice intruded on her daydreaming.

She turned to see him leaning against the table near Ruth's bed, an unfathomable expression on his face.

"Hullo Chris! How nice to see you. You've been missed by all and sundry! Welcome back! I hope your latest trip was successful."

Doctor Maynard's mission over the past few weeks had been chasing up building supplies for the new clinic, a job taking far more time than he'd anticipated. Having to travel to the sources seemed to be the only way to ensure delivery, which meant being away from The Haven for days at a time. The doctor had a greater understanding of the word frustration.

"Yes it was. Hopefully productive, but I'd like a word with you, Penny. Have you time to put your duties on hold for a few minutes? I need to discuss something with you."

"Of course. I'll let Sister Mercy know."

"She knows. I've just come from asking her permission to whisk you away for five minutes. Amazingly, she needed no persuading."

I'm sure she didn't, thought Penny wryly, knowing Sister Mercy was still convinced Chris fancied her. If he did, he had a funny way of showing it, as there had been little contact between them since the snake affair.

Penny was surprised at how much she missed having him pop into the ward, but deliberately banished the thoughts as soon as they appeared. She knew Clair felt very strongly about the doctor.

Clair!

Penny wasn't sure about Clair anymore.

There was an undercurrent emanating from the nurse that bothered her. Nothing she could put her finger on, a suggestion of hostility maybe, although outwardly, Clair was as friendly as ever. In fact, even more so.

Maybe that's it, thought Penny. *She's being too friendly and it feels false, somehow.*

Doctor Maynard glanced down at Penny as they walked towards the baobab tree, concerned at seeing the troubled expression on her face. Nothing and nobody must cause his nurse to have any other look except one of happiness.

"Hey, Penny. Don't look so anxious. I promise you're not in any sort of trouble."

Penny laughed, the frown disappearing as she looked up at the doctor.

"I'm sorry. I was far away then. What is it you want to discuss?"

They'd reached the baobab tree and were sitting on the garden chairs placed in its shade.

"Well, I'm arranging an expedition into the interior looking for potential leprosy sufferers. I know that sounds a bit strange, but if a villager shows any signs of the disease, he or she is banished from the village and housed in a hut built a distance away from the rest. The other villagers bring food for the sufferer, but leave it a good distance from the hut, because they're obviously scared of getting the disease. You can imagine the lonely existence these poor people go through."

Chris stopped speaking, memories flooding into his mind of patients he'd found living solitary lives, with no human contact whatsoever, barely existing.

He cleared his throat and continued talking.

"I wondered if you would like to come along. I've spoken to Sister Magdalene and Sister Mercy, and they both felt it would be a good idea. You have the knack of building up a good rapport with the Ugandans. They like and trust you."

Doctor Maynard looked at Penny carefully.

"You'd be surprised at how well known you are outside this colony. You're not known as the dove for nothing."

Penny looked at the doctor in amazement. How did he know about the nickname she'd been given?

Chris laughed. "Don't look so shocked, Penny. Even though I haven't been around these last few weeks, there's not much happening I don't know about. And anyway, the name you've been given is entirely suitable. I couldn't have picked a better one myself," *except maybe to put darling before it*, he added silently.

"So, does the trip appeal to you? We'll be away for about a week to ten days. Tents will be the order of the day, almost like going on safari, except we shall be hunting people rather than animals, metaphorically speaking of course."

"Oh, absolutely! I would love to. Who else will be going? Will Clair be coming along?"

Not if I can help it, thought the doctor.

"No, I shouldn't think so. She'll probably go on the next trip. I'm sure Sister Magdalene wouldn't like both of you leaving together. Sisters Margaret and Mary will be coming, as they've been on a few of these expeditions before, and of course, David, Thomas and Joseph. Both Joseph and Thomas can drive, so they'll have a land

41

rover each and I'll drive one. We'll have plenty of room if we find any potential patients."

Chris stopped talking and looked intently into Penny's eyes. He'd missed her so much. Life lost its sparkle, its magic if he couldn't see her everyday. How frustrating to spend so much time in Jinja when all he really wanted was to be at The Haven to get passing glimpses of his darling as she walked to and fro from the ward. How he missed the times he ate lunch and dinner with her, just being able to feast his eyes on her face as she spoke about the happenings of the day. *Did she think of me at all whilst I was away*, he wondered. *She appeared please to see me when I returned. But am I reading more into that because I want to?* He smiled, a rather sheepish smile and said, "I'm looking forward to showing you the beauty of the Ugandan bush. I just love this country, and to share it with the, well, to be able to show you its enchantment."

He stopped talking. *Blast it! Pull yourself together, for goodness sake,* he admonished himself.

Penny smiled at the doctor. "I couldn't imagine anyone I would prefer to show me the wonders of Uganda", surprised at how much she meant it.

She looked away quickly, blushing in confusion, but not before he saw the tell tell colour creeping up her neck and into her cheeks.

I do believe you're making progress, Chris my boy. A week in the bush, nights spent under the African moon can only enhance your chances. Keep playing your cards right and she will be yours.

And with that last heartening thought, he escorted Penny back to the ward.

CHAPTER SIX

Clair was not a happy bunny.

She was frustrated at the amount of time Chris was away from The Haven.

"How can I get him to notice me if he's never here," she muttered, yanking a sheet tight. "Even when he is here, he only has eyes for simpering Penny, and she makes out she doesn't even notice. I will make him love me," she vowed, as she quickly tidied the bed and moved down the ward to the next one. "I just need to get her out of the way permanently"

"Did you here what I said, Nurse Dansbury?"

Clair jumped and saw Sister Angelica standing at the foot of the bed.

"I'm sorry, Sister. No, I didn't."

"When you've finished with this bed, please go to Sister Mercy and ask if she has any spare dressings we could use until the supplies arrive. I know we use more on this ward, so she might be able to give us some."

"Yes, of course," said Clair, and quickly tucked in the sheets before walking next door to the women's ward.

That's when she saw Penny and the doctor sitting under the baobab tree.

Resentment and rage swept through her body like a raging torrent.

"The little bitch!" she muttered vehemently. "As soon as he arrives back from Jinja, there's simpering Penny getting her claws into him.

She says one thing but does the opposite. How stupid does she think I am? Well Miss Penny goody shoes, the doctor will find out what a nasty piece of work you are under that angelic exterior, if it's the last thing I do!"

She knelt down to supposedly retie a wayward shoe- lace whilst furtively watching Doctor Maynard escort Penny back to the ward.

Yes, I must put my plan into action, and from the look of things, there's no time to lose.

Clair hurried across the courtyard and entered the women's ward in time to see the doctor wave to Penny as he turned to leave. Clair positioned herself causing Chris to bump into her as though by accident.

"I'm sorry Clair. I didn't see you behind me."

"That's O.K. Chris. Did you have a good time in Jinja? I missed seeing you around. Are you here for good now?"

"Well, the building supplies are back on tract for the new clinic, but I've been told there is a weeks delay. However, that time is being put to good use. An expedition into the interior is due, so Penny will be coming along as we look for people suffering from leprosy."

Chris stopped talking. He could've kicked himself. As soon as he mentioned Penny's name he knew he'd made a mistake. He felt rather than saw a change come over Clair. She was still smiling but there was a difference, as though she was finding it difficult to keep the smile on her face.

"Oh, so Penny will be tagging along, will she? Any chance I can join the trip as well? I would love to see more of Uganda, and this will be an ideal way of doing it."

The doctor was in a quandary. The last thing he wanted was Clair taking up Penny time, but how to let her down easily without hurting her feelings.

"I think Sister Magdalene would prefer you to go on the next one. She wouldn't be happy if both of you left The Haven at the same time."

We'll see about that, thought Clair, as she shrugged her shoulders and said, "Never mind. Next time will be fine," and left Chris standing in the middle of the ward as she went to ask Sister Mercy about the dressings.

Doctor Maynard felt uneasy.

Clair agreed much too readily, he thought, walking across the courtyard to his office. However, the office phone was ringing, and soon he was in discussions with a building supplier who disagreed with the specifications he'd quoted. Clair was erased from the doctor's mind.

The nurse, meanwhile, was busy scheming as she renewed a hand dressing on one of her patients.

The first thing I must do is persuade Sister Magdalene to let me go on the trip. I have to discredit Penny in such a way Chris will wonder what on earth he saw in her. But how to talk Sister Magdalene around? What story can I tell convincing her I must go?

The nurse finished cutting the last piece of tape holding the dressing together. Her green eyes glistened as she dismissed the patient. The audacious idea, the seeds of which had been festering in her mind since that first evening at the Haven came flooding back. The scheme was so appealing in its wickedness she knew she had to use it. Her mind flashed back to that first evening, when she determined to get rid of her rival, and now the first real prospect to put that plan into action was at hand.

Dare I do it? Oh yes, absolutely!

Clair's opportunity came that evening.

She saw Mother Superior walking along the corridor towards the dining room, and hurried to catch up with her.

"Sister Magdalene, can I have a word with you, please. It's rather private."

"Of course, Clair. Shall we go to my office?"

The nurse agreed, and once settled in a chair facing the nun, she proceeded to put her plan into action.

"It's like this, Sister Magdalene. Penny has told me she's been invited to join the expedition to the interior looking for people suffering from leprosy."

She paused, as though reluctant to continue talking.

"Yes, Clair. That's correct."

"Well, Penny has told me something, Sister Magdalene, in confidence. But I felt you should know what she is saying, because frankly, it doesn't make any sense."

Again Clair paused to show her unwillingness in speaking out of turn.

"Please Clair, if you have something to say which you believe I should know, then just say it."

"Well, Penny said she's worried about being on her own with Doctor Maynard. She said she would feel much happier if I went along. I said I thought she was being silly. I mean, Doctor Maynard wouldn't hurt a fly, but she was really insistent, Sister Magdalene. I asked her if anything had happened to make her feel that way, but she wouldn't elaborate. All she would say was she really wished I could join her, because she would feel much safer."

Clair looked at Mother Superior, who sat speechless, astonishment showing on her face.

"Please don't say anything to Penny, Sister Magdalene. She told me this in confidence, and I don't want her to think I can't keep my mouth shut. But, if you could see your way clear to letting me go as well, I know Penny would appreciate that very much."

Mother Superior was briefly at a loss for words, probably for the first time in her life.

"Really Clair! Are you saying that Penny is frightened of Doctor Maynard? I find that hard to believe. When I've seen them together they look so relaxed in each other's company. Are you sure you haven't misunderstood what you've been told?"

"Oh, believe me, Sister Magdalene, I said the same to Penny, but all she would say is the doctor is not all that he seems."

"Well, let me think about it. I'll let you know in the morning," and Sister Magdalene stood up, indicating the interview was over.

As Clair moved to open the door, she said again, "Please don't say anything to Penny. She would be devastated to think I couldn't hold my tongue."

The nurse paused, as though again wanting to say more, but appearing unwilling to continue.

"If there is anything further, please say it Clair. Nothing that is spoken in this office goes any further."

"I've noticed Penny fantasises a lot. She exaggerates things. Penny likes drama in her life, and if there isn't any, she'll make it up. I'm sure she doesn't mean any harm, Sister Magdalene. In fact, Penny probably doesn't even know she's doing it, but I've got to know her well since we've been at The Haven, and I've caught her out quite a few times lying about things."

Clair opened the door.

"I know I can leave this matter in your hands, Sister Magdalene. Thank you so much for sparing the time to listen to me. I like Penny. You know you can trust me to look out for her," and on that parting shot, Clair left the office, feeling well satisfied with her evenings work.

Mother Superior stayed sitting at her desk, a bewildered look on her face as she thought about the things Clair had told her.

Maybe I don't know Penny as well as I thought I did. Has she got a serious psychological problem none of us are aware of? To accuse poor Doctor Maynard of misconduct. This is very worrying. Perhaps it would be a good thing for Clair to go on the trip.

The nun rested her head in her hands.

It would be appalling if Doctor Maynard were put into a compromising situation. His reputation would be in tatters. It's very kind of Clair to look out for Penny. Yes. Clair must go with them. I shall tell her in the morning.

Sister Magdalene sighed, decided to skip dinner and go to her room. She needed to go on her knees for a while.

The next morning Clair could hardly contain herself.

Sister Magdalene had just told her she would be going on the trip, and she couldn't wait to tell Penny the good news.

"Now I really will be able to put a spanner in the works," she gloated quietly to herself, whilst hurrying to the baobab tree to have fruit juice with the nurse during their morning break.

"We'll see what Miss high and mighty has to say about this."

Penny was already waiting for her.

"I've got your juice, Clair. Freshly squeezed mango. I do believe this is my favourite out of all the ones we've tried. Mind you, the pineapple concoction comes a close second," and smiled happily at her friend as Clair sat in the garden chair opposite her.

"You'll never guess what's happened, Penny. Sister Magdalene called me into her office this morning, and told me I'll also be going on the expedition. Isn't that great? She said that as our patient numbers are less, the workload would be down quite a bit, so the nuns will be able to manage without the both of us for a week. I'm really excited."

Penny's first initial reaction was dismay, but then she admonished herself for what she thought was her selfishness, and said, "that's great Clair. It will be lovely to have you come along. I'm sure Chris will be delighted."

Chris was not delighted, in fact he was furious, but struggling hard to keep his feelings under control, as Sister Magdalene continued speaking.

"I just think it would be better if both nurses went. We are quiet at the moment, having discharged a large number of patients, so this is the ideal time for both Penny and Clair to venture into the interior and experience for themselves what goes on in the bush. Anyway, they will be good company for each other. You know it isn't easy, especially for women."

"I'm quite capable of looking after Penny, Sister Magdalene."

"Do you think I don't know that? Of course I do. I just feel it would be better if both girls went."

Mother Superior hesitated, as though there was something she wanted to add, but then had second thoughts.

"Is there anything else before I go?" asked the doctor.

"No, I believe that's all. I'm sure you'll have a successful time, but Chris, please be careful."

"I always am, Sister Magdalene. Now, I think I'd better get things organised. I hope to leave day after tomorrow," and he strode out of Mother Superior's office, calm outside, but inwardly frustrated.

Well, I'll just have to get used to the idea of Clair joining us. I almost feel as though Sister Magdalene is sending her along as chaperone. But regardless, I'm sure there'll be opportunities to get Penny on her own, and on that heartening thought, the doctor returned to his office to organise food, tents, essential equipment, medicines and a thousand and one other things needed to spend a week or so in the African bush.

Clair, meanwhile, was gloating.

She returned to her ward to help feed patients their lunch, her mind busy forming and rejecting tactics to discredit Penny further.

I mustn't be obvious. Mother Superior believes I'm her good friend, and that I only have her best interests at heart. There's bound to be opportunities on the trip I can use to further my plan. I need to turn Chris against her, but I'll have to be very subtle about it, drop a few hints here and there and be ready to grasp and use any situation that may occur to show Penny in a bad light."

The nurse grinned to herself and said softly, "This is going to be such fun. I will take her down, and at the same time, snare the doctor. Oh, yes, Chris. We are going to be so happy together, you and I."

"Careful, Nurse Dansbury! There's more food going down the front of Zechariah than in his mouth."

Sister Angelica's voice held a certain measure of censure.

"Gosh! I'm sorry Sister. I wasn't concentrating," and Clair continued feeding the patient carefully, but unable to stop her devious mind picturing Penny's downfall, and Clair herself, comforting the devastated doctor after he realised that his precious Penny was anything but that.

Chapter Seven

They were packed and ready to go; three land rovers lined up, one behind the other in the driveway of the courtyard, Doctor Maynard in the driving seat of the first one, Clair sitting next to him, (how she'd wrangled that, Chris didn't know) and Penny in the back. Sisters Margaret and Mary were in the next land rover driven by Joseph, and Thomas brought up the rear.

All staff and those patients who could manage it, crowded around the courtyard to give them a rousing send off.

"Ready ladies?" asked Chris, and he turned in his seat to look at Penny.

She smiled and nodded.

"Good. Let's go," and he slowly released the clutch and the vehicle moved forward.

Clair and Penny waved until The Haven was no longer in sight, and then settled back to enjoy the ride.

It had been a hectic few days getting everything ready, including writing letters home warning families they would be out of reach for at least a week. Although they had their mobile phones, Chris couldn't guarantee reception where they were going.

Penny leant back in her seat, looking out of the window, a slight frown on her face.

She was baffled.

What is it? she wondered, as they bumped along the dirt track leading to the main road to Jinja. *Why do I feel an atmosphere, an undercurrent gaining momentum? I even felt it emanating from Mother*

Superior. She gave herself a mental shake. *You are imagining things, Penny Whickam, so stop being silly and enjoy what lies ahead.*

This was the first time the girls had been to Jinja, although Chris skirted the town rather than going through it.

The township lies on the shores of Lake Victoria and is full of old Asian style buildings, reflecting the days when Jinja had a sizeable Asian community. The town was virtually owned by Asians until Idi Amin kicked them out in the early seventies. Many, though, were now returning and the town was becoming prosperous again, after falling into disarray and ruin.

One claim to fame it does have, is that Jinja is one of the spots Mahatma Ghandi chose to have some of his ashes scattered.

The town is close to the Owen Falls Dam where a hydroelectric station has been built supplying Uganda with the bulk of its electricity. The main Kampala to Jinja road runs across the top of the dam, Jinja lying about 60km northeast of Kampala.

Having passed the town, Chris branched off right and soon they were back on dirt roads. Penny felt as though she were in paradise, her head swivelling backwards and forwards not wanting to miss anything of this tropical enchantment.

Chris watched her in his rear view mirror; delighted at the interest she took in the country he now called home.

"If you look carefully, Penny, you might see buck hiding in the bush. There are plenty of antelopes including eland, kudu, bushbuck and impala. And the birds are amazing. Did you know Uganda has 1008 bird species recorded within its borders? This place is a bird watchers paradise."

"I love bird watching," said Clair, desperately wanting Chris's attention for herself.

It didn't work. She felt rather than saw the looks the doctor continually gave the rear view mirror as he took fleeting glances at Penny, seeing with pleasure, emotions of wonder and amazement sweep across her face at the sights she was witnessing. *Penny's fallen in love with this country*, Chris thought with satisfaction.

Driving near the banks of a river, Chris cautioned the girls about Nile crocodiles found in most rivers and lakes in Uganda.

"They are huge and can move with the most amazing speed. Do not, I repeat, do not go close to any river without an armed guard protecting you. And of course, lion, leopard, cheetah plus jackals and African hunting dogs are also present, so no wandering off by your-selves. The African bush can look deceptively harmless, but you never know what dangers are lurking, especially during the mating and birthing seasons."

They stopped, allowing a troop of baboons meander across the dirt track, babies clinging to their mother's backs as they foraged for insects, fruit and anything else taking their fancy.

"All we need now is Tarzan howling as he comes swinging in," said Clair, "and the picture will be complete!"

Penny chuckled as Chris continued their education. "Uganda is presently the best location for tracking mountain gorillas. That's an experience not to be missed, so during the course of your stay, we'll make a plan to do just that, if you want to, that is," and he glanced in the mirror to gauge Penny's response.

He was not disappointed.

Beautiful eyes shining with excitement, an enduring smile on her face, she met his glance and said, "I would love to. I just love it all," believing life couldn't get any better…

The nurses were sitting around the blazing campfire, opposite the nuns, quietly talking. They'd made camp for the night in a clearing, and after helping pitch tents and collect fire -wood, were now drinking coffee whilst enjoying the sounds of nocturnal animals reverberating through the bush. Joseph, designated chef as well as driver, had done a sterling job, cooking up a sumptuous meal of barbecued steaks enhanced with salad and mango, washed down with freshly ground coffee.

"What a delicious meal," said Clair, and leant back in her fold up chair. "Who would've thought we'd be eating so grandly in the middle of the bush."

She paused, and then looked at her companion.

"You're very quiet, Penny. Is anything wrong?"

"Nothing at all, Clair. I'm just enjoying the moment. However, although it seems so peaceful, I know that's just an illusion. Under cover of darkness, the predators are out and about hunting down their supper."

She gave an involuntary shiver.

"Somebody walking over your grave?" asked Clair. "You must be careful, Penny. You never know what's lurking behind the next bush in a place like this. One moment you're feeling snug and secure in your little world, and the next, wham!" and she made a chopping motion with her hand.

"That's enough Clair!"

Chris Maynard's voice sounded out of the darkness, and he strode into view, the light from the fire illuminating the stern expression on his face.

"I've checked the perimeter of our camp and everything is as it should be." He walked over to Penny and laid a hand on her shoulder.

"You're perfectly safe with me. You know you've nothing to worry about."

She smiled up at him. "I know that Chris. I'm fine, really I am."

"Good," and then the doctor called Joseph to replenish their coffee.

"We'll have an early night tonight as I want to be on the road by eight tomorrow morning. We need to be at Kangabuta by lunchtime. I know the chief of that village well. We should get some information regarding any prospective patients in his area."

Sisters Margaret and Mary said their goodnights and headed off to their tents.

Penny smiled her thanks as Joseph poured more coffee into her waiting mug. She slowly sipped the steaming liquid whilst staring into the flickering flames of the campfire. All talk ceased as each member of the team disappeared into their own thoughts; Chris admiring the highlighted contours of Penny's face bathed in the glow from the fire, wishing he could run his fingers over her brow, down pass her cheekbones and eventually reach those luscious lips; Penny realising with relief thinking of her former fiancé and her best friend together didn't cause her nearly as much heartache as it used to; Clair artfully spinning webs of intrigue and deceit in her mind, thinking up ways to permantly discredit Penny, causing Chris to look upon his former love with disgust and loathing. Seeing Chris touching the nurse's shoulder had infuriated her. *I deserve his caresses, not that conniving Nurse Whickam.*

Once again Penny shivered, bringing her back to the present. A sensation of foreboding hung over her, spoiling the ambience of the moment.

I'm just tired, she thought. *A good night's sleep is needed.*

"I think its time to say goodnight," she announced. "I'll see you both in the morning. Sleep well," and the nurse melted away into the darkness, the beam from her torch illuminating the way to her tent.

The doctor made a move to rise.

"Wait Chris. Don't go yet," said Clair, grasping at the opportunity presenting itself to spread a little mischief.

"There's something I must tell you, something I feel you need to know."

Chris paused, and then with an inward sigh said, "What's on your mind, Clair?"

"Well…it's about Penny."

Chris stiffened in his chair.

"What about her?"

"I'm not sure how to say this, but did you know she's a little scared of you?"

"What! Scared of me? Don't be ridiculous. Where did you get such a ludicrous idea from?"

"Oh, it hasn't come from me. No, it was Mother Superior who hinted at it. I was really surprised when she asked me to go on this trip as I would've been quite content to go on the next one, but Sister Magdalene implied she thought it would be better for Penny to have me come along as she would feel safer somehow. Does that make any sense to you? I can't believe you've done anything to Penny to make her scared of you?"

"Of course I haven't. I don't know where Sister Magdalene could've got that idea."

The doctor's mind went back to the conversation he'd had with Mother Superior and the feeling Clair was along the trip as chaperone.

Clair broke the silence.

"Anyway Chris, I thought it best to mention this so you would understand why Penny may be reluctant to be on her own with you. I know it's all in her mind. You would never do anything untoward, I know that."

The nurse looked at the uncertainty playing over the doctor's face, and decided she'd said enough for now.

Let him digest that titbit for starters, she thought, and rose from her chair, one hand supposedly smothering a yawn, but then couldn't resist stoking the fires just a little more.

"I'm off to bed. Don't worry Chris. I'll make sure Penny doesn't cause any trouble. I do like her. I think her mind can be a little fanciful," and on that note, Clair switched on her torch and disappeared into the darkness.

Chris stayed where he was, staring into the campfire, his mind running round in circles as he tried to make sense of what Clair had said.

There's some mistake. There has to be. No way have I done anything to make Penny frightened of me, and she certainly hasn't acted in any way to make me think that she is. Oh, it's just nonsense. Mother Superior is being over protective, that's all, and I bet Clair has exaggerated what she said, so, nothing is going to spoil this trip, least of all, a bit of hearsay.

CHAPTER EIGHT

Penny slept soundly; blissfully unaware of the destructive seeds Clair so enjoyed sowing. Now and again she'd been woken by the bark of baboons but quickly slipped back into sleep.

She was dressed and sitting by the now smouldering campfire, sipping the delicious coffee Joseph had given her, when the doctor ambled into view.

"Good morning Chris. What a beautiful morning this is," and smiled happily up at him.

The doctor's heart lurched in his chest as he gazed down at her upturned face.

Sister Magdalene is totally wrong about Penny, he thought, as he acknowledged her good morning, and thanked Joseph for the mug of coffee.

He looked at the nurse, hands shielding her eyes from the glare, as she stared into the distance, admiring the effects of the suns rays on the foliage.

No one as beautiful and as kind and compassionate as Penny could think and say such hurtful things. It's all a huge misunderstanding, and he smiled at her as she turned to him and whispered, "Look Chris. Can you see that brightly coloured parrot in that tree over there," and as she pointed, Chris leant closer to get a better look, and that's when Clair arrived, in a foul mood anyway because she hadn't slept well, which promptly changed to outright hostility as she thought she saw her doctor about to embrace her enemy.

"Good morning," she called out loudly, causing Chris to move quickly away from Penny, who cried out in consternation as the startled parrot flew away in a flurry of scarlet feathers.

"Oh, I'm sorry," said Clair. "Did I disturb something?"

"I was showing Chris this beautiful parrot in the thorn tree over there. Never mind Clair, you didn't know. Did you sleep well?"

"No problem," and she reached out to receive her mug of coffee from Joseph's proffered hand. "And you Chris? Did you have a good night?"

"Fine," was his reply and bent over the fire to give the embers a stir with his boot. "Joseph's bringing our breakfast and then we'll strike camp and be on our way."

Penny was surprised at his brusqueness.

Gone was the commradie she'd so enjoyed, to be replaced with an atmosphere brittle and spiky. Again she shivered, feelings of foreboding sweeping through her body. *What is going on? Why do I keep feeling like this?*

Clair didn't appear to notice anything.

She sat in her chair, chatting away about inconsequential things until Joseph arrived with porridge and powdered scrambled eggs followed by fresh fruit. The nuns put in an appearance, and once breakfast was eaten, everyone helped to strike camp and by 8am they were in the land rovers on their way to Kangabuta, Clair having manoeuvred her way again to sit next to Chris. He couldn't say anything without sounding churlish, so contented himself with frequent glances at his love in the rear view mirror.

Penny was unaware of the surreptitious looks given by the doctor, her eyes firmly fixed on the passing bush, struggling to quell the feelings of apprehension rising up in her.

This is nonsense, Penny. Stop it! You're spoiling the trip for yourself, and the others will notice if you don't snap out of it. Concentrate on the beauty you're seeing. This is a once in a life- time experience, my girl. Just enjoy it!

They drove along dirt roads for an hour before Chris pointed to a large clearing, which had at least a dozen thatched huts dotted all over.

"There's Kangabuta, ladies. I'll speak to the chief and see what information I can get."

Kangabuta was a typical African village of around a dozen daub and wattle straw covered huts with scrawny chickens squabbling over dropped titbits as women sat on their haunches bent over stone slabs grinding corn from mealies or corn on the cob to make flour. Goats nibbled desultory at anything of interest as young women walked with plastic buckets full of water balanced on their heads from the river to their huts. Young men were overseeing their cattle, keeping an eye out for predators, whilst old men sat on wooden stools, backs leant against the clay walls of their huts reminiscing on times past as they sucked hard on clay pipes filled with home grown tobacco.

Small naked children ran towards the convoy chattering and laughing. As Chris climbed out of the land rover, they grabbed his hands and led him to where Chief Tazwhila was standing by his hut. The doctor extended his hand to the welcoming chief.

"We are overjoyed to see you again, Doctor Maynard," said Chief Tazwhila, resplendent in leopard skin robes and a head dress made of ostrich plumes, "and the two nurses from England we have heard so much about. This one must be the dove," smiling at Penny, causing the nurse to stare in amazement before remembering her manners and swiftly dropping her eyes. Looking straight in the eyes of an African when being addressed is taboo and considered very discourteous.

Clair seethed inwardly.

She won't be known as the dove by the time I finish with her. More like the scorpion with a sting in her tail, and then smiled sweetly at the chief who had extended his hand in greeting.

"Come, let us drink sorghum together and you will tell me why you have paid us a visit to our humble village," and he clapped his hands, whereby small wooden three legged stools were swiftly brought by young maidens of the tribe and wooden bowls with a thick white liquid handed to the guests.

Penny sipped the bitter tasting liquid, trying hard not to make a face as it hit the back of her throat.

"This is strong stuff," she whispered to Clair. "One bowl of this and I'll be on my ear," and she quietly placed the bowl beside her stool. Clair did the same, but the doctor drank all of his and then stood up and made a short speech thanking the chief and the villagers for their hospitality. Then he got down to the main business of their visit.

"Chief Tazwhila, as you are aware, we are always on the lookout for villagers affected by leprosy, so we can take them back to the clinic for treatment. Do you know of anybody who needs our help?"

"We have been fortunate here, Doctor Maynard. All my people are healthy, thanks to your education programmes. No, I believe you will need to travel further into the interior. I have heard there are a few sick people near Mr. Angus McFadden's coffee plantation. I am surprise he has not told you himself."

Doctor Maynard swore under his breath.

Angus McFadden was the last person on this earth he wanted to visit.

CHAPTER NINE

Angus McFadden sat in his favourite wicker chair on the open veranda of the Anglisa Coffee Plantation homestead, staring into the distance.

The view was spectacular.

The deep blue of a cloudless sky made a perfect backdrop for rows upon rows of coffee bushes stretching into the distance, the deep lime green of foliage contrasting vividly with bunches of yellow-orange coffee beans. The gentle humming of a rhythmic propensity emanated from the bent backs of coffee pickers making their way along the rows of bushes, baskets straining under the weight of their cargo.

But Angus McFadden was in no mood to appreciate the view. Pure, undiluted crimson anger misted his eyes preventing him from seeing anything other than his own inward torment.

So, that bastard Maynard is in the area. News travels fast through the bush; quicker than any telephone.

He leant forward, resting his elbows on his knees, contemplating the laces in his scuffed, well worn leather boots.

Still on his goodwill missions, no doubt, the lying bastard. How he can gallivant around the country as though he hasn't a care in the world is beyond me.

The Scotsman stood, stretched and then walked up and down the veranda, wooden boards creaking in protest as his heavy boots beat out a staccato rhythm.

He mustn't come here. I'll set my dogs on him, so help me I will.

The rapid pacing came to a halt, and the plantation owner slowly lowered his lean, sinewy body back into the chair once more.

The hatred receded, replaced with an emptiness all-encompassing, inside and out, an emptiness so profound, so void of feeling and thought, he felt as though he were existing inside a vacuum. Cindy, a Staffordshire terrier and his favourite dog, sensing her master's anguish, rubbed her cold muzzle into the palm of his hand.

The contact with a living being shattered the vacuum, and heat raced through his body again, the heat of deep-seated rage and loathing.

I will make you pay, Doctor Bloody Maynard. Somehow I will make you pay for destroying my life when you took my Lisa from me.

Not able to stop himself, his mind flew back to the day, the very moment when Lisa died in his arms.

"Don't blame Chris," she whispered, defending Maynard right up to the end. "He didn't know, Angus!" She clutched his arm with her last remaining strength. "Angus, he tried his best. I love you," and then she shuddered and was gone. His Lisa, his darling Lisa. The only person he'd ever loved and would ever love. His sweet, gentle loving Lisa. Gone for all eternity.

He remembered the first time he laid eyes on his soul mate.

It was in his native Scotland, and he was striding along a mountain track in the highlands on a glorious autumn morning, indulging his love of mountaineering, when he heard a faint call for help. Answering the call, he tracked the voice down to a ridge on the mountainside, and there was Lisa, her long, blond hair escaping her woolly hat, as she waved her arms like a windmill to attract his attention. "I'm down here," she yelled, her voice echoing his Scottish burr. One glance showed her ankle wedged between two rocks. She was obviously in a lot of pain, but managed to give a crooked grin and said, "My knight in shining armour has finally arrived."

He said, "You're a daft lassie," and that was it.

He was head over heels in love in an instance. By the time he'd freed her from the rocks, strapped her ankle and helped her down the mountainside, he knew this was the woman he wanted to be with for the rest of his life. Her sense of adventure complimented his, and when the opportunity arose for Angus to purchase a coffee plantation in Uganda, she was full of enthusiasm for the venture, immersing herself in the country and its culture, loving the people, who in turn, loved her. She was everything to Angus and his life ended when she died.

He remembered turning his head to confront Chris Maynard.

The doctor spoke. "I'm so sorry Angus. I did everything I could, but you do have..."

"Get out. Get out before I throw you out. Call yourself a doctor! You let my Lisa die, you bastard. You let my Lisa die! GET OUT! GET OUT!" he screamed, his overwhelming grief exacerbated with hatred. "GET OUT!"

The memories exhausted him. He slumped back in his chair; gut wrenching sobs shaking his body as though overwhelmed with fever.

Cindy whimpered and fretted, front paws now resting on his knees as she tried to lick his face to comfort him.

"It's O.K. Cindy," he whispered, stroking her head. "It's O.K. I'll get my revenge. I've spent too long in the past. Now it's time to even the score. Revenge is sweet, so they say. Let me taste that sweetness. Let me destroy the doctor's life like he destroyed mine. Then maybe this existence called living will be slightly more bearable to handle."

He paced the veranda again, this time slowly; unknowing fate was already preparing the way for him.

CHAPTER TEN

The party were sat in a semi circle on Angus McFadden's veranda. The atmosphere was tense, undercurrents of hostility simmering under polite conversation.

Chris Maynard had reluctantly decided to call on his former friend. After all, maybe there were potential patients needing treatment. Admittedly, it was a visit he could've done without but it had to be done. Their long- standing feud must not jeopardise the work he'd undertaken. The doctor took Penny and Clair along to act as icebreakers, and so far, that part of the plan was working, not brilliantly but at least Angus hadn't kicked them out.

Clair sat quietly, her brain going into overdrive. *There's history between Angus McFadden and Chris. I can sense it, and if I'm not mistaken, it isn't a nice history. The tension between the two is tangible. Oh yes, politenesses like icing covering a ticking time bomb. I wonder what it's all about? Could this be the chance I've been waiting for, a time bomb whose fuse I could light, and get Penny blasted by the fallout? Could this be my opportunity to remove the dear, delightful dove from the scene?* She smiled her thanks as Molly, the house girl, handed her a cup of tea.

At least Angus didn't set his dogs on me, Chris thought, his gaze resting on Penny as she asked the plantation owner about his dog Cindy.

"She's clearly devoted to you. Have you had her long?"

"My wife Lisa gave her to me on our third wedding anniversary. Lisa is dead," and with that declaration, Angus glared at the doctor.

Chris felt his body stiffen, and then waited, without surprise, for what he knew was forth coming.

Penny noticed the look and was taken aback at the animosity she felt directed at Chris.

"I'm so sorry," she said. "You obviously miss her very much."

"More than anybody will ever know."

"May I ask what happened to your wife, or would you rather not talk about it?" and then immediately regretted the question.

"You don't need to ask me, Penny. Just speak to the good doctor here. He'll tell you all about it, won't you Doctor Maynard? After all, you killed her, didn't you? DIDN'T YOU?" and Angus stood up and stormed away from the veranda.

There was a stunned silence.

Penny, mortified, a stricken look on her face, stared at the doctor. Clair was the first to speak.

"Well done Penny. You put both feet in good and proper."

Dr Maynard sprang to his love's defence.

"That's enough Clair. Penny had no idea about Lisa," and strode over to the horrified nurse, putting his arm around her shoulders. She sat, still as a statue, a frozen look of disbelief on her face.

"Oh Chris, I'm so sorry. How could I have been so tactless? That poor man. You could feel his torment. But how could he accuse you of killing his wife?" Penny looked up into Chris's face. "What a terrible thing to say."

"Yes, well, grief can make people say things they wouldn't normally voice. Lisa died just over a year ago. Angus loved her very much and took her death extremely hard. He hasn't come to terms with it yet."

Chris took Penny by the arm. "Don't worry. Its time we went back to camp anyway. Clair, are you coming?" and he helped the shaken nurse down the wooden stairs of the homestead, to where the land rover was parked in the driveway.

Clair had to know more, and making an excuse to fetch her bag from inside the house, hurried to find the plantation owner. Angus was staring out of the lounge window, sucking heavily on his pipe.

Clair walked quietly up to the man and laid a hand on his arm. Angus started, turned to look at the nurse and then resumed looking out of the window.

"What do you want?" he asked.

"Can I visit you again Angus? We might be able to help each other."

"What do you mean?" he asked abruptly. "I don't need help. I need justice. Look, go back to your friends. Just leave me alone, please."

Clair didn't move.

After a couple of minutes, Angus relented.

"I'm sorry. I'm being boorish. Of course you can visit," and then he left the room, leaving Clair exhilarated with potential possibilities flying through her mind.

She hurried out to the land rover.

"Sorry to keep you waiting. My bag was by my chair all the time," and she scrambled into the vehicle, this time content to sit in the back, already scheming how to visit Angus at the earliest possibility.

They were back at camp, sitting round the fire, sparks from the glowing logs shooting into the air like crazed fire- flies. The distant calls of hyenas echoed around the perimeter, their high- pitched howls emphasising the isolation of the group.

Penny felt distraught. She couldn't get the look of despair in Angus's face out of her mind. Why did he accuse Chris of killing his wife? What did he mean? How could someone like Dr Maynard kill anyone? Did Lisa have an accident and Chris couldn't save her, or was she suffering from an illness that killed her and in his grief, Angus blamed Chris for not healing her?

Penny glanced over to where the doctor was sitting, leaning forward, hands cupping his chin as he stared into the flames of the fire, deep in thought.

I don't know how to comfort him, she thought, surprised at the overwhelming need in her of wanting to do just that. *Goodness! What a mess I made of things. Why couldn't I keep my mouth shut?*

Chris Maynard sat back in his chair and then stood up. "I'm off to bed. We have an early start tomorrow. Goodnight ladies," and disappeared into the darkness.

Clair was working on a plan to visit Angus without the other two knowing.

I'll have to play hooky. I'll make up some cock and bull tale tomorrow morning so I can stay at the camp. When everybody has left, I'll visit Angus McFadden and get the story out of him. I can walk to his place in half an hour. It's a wide, well used dirt road; I shouldn't be in any danger from wild animals. It's no good asking Chris what caused the outburst. He clams up when Angus's name is mentioned.

She smiled to herself.

This opportunity is too good to miss. I know I can work it to my advantage somehow. The oh so dutiful Penny is feeling terrible at stirring up a hornet's nest. She'll be putty in my hands if I can suggest a way for her to make things better.

Clair yawned loudly, whilst walking over to Penny, who was still sitting, absorbed in her thoughts. She put her arms around the nurse and gave her a hug.

"I'm off to bed as well, Penny. Not a nice ending to a tiring day, but don't blame yourself too much. I'm sure things will work out."

"You're right, Clair. Beating myself up isn't helping anybody. Sleep well. I'll see you in the morning."

Penny sat by the fire for a little longer, her thoughts divided between Chris and Angus. So much hatred from Angus towards the doctor. And Chris? Penny didn't know what Chris felt. He refused to be drawn on the subject and Penny respected his privacy, although Clair had tried to push it until the doctor told her abruptly to leave it alone.

The intense yearning she felt to comfort him. Where did that come from? Most likely feeling so guilty at being the cause of the upset. She wanted to make amends, but would an opportunity present itself?

Oh well, I may as well go to bed. Brooding like this isn't helping. Let's see what tomorrow brings.

CHAPTER ELEVEN

The morning dawned crisp and fresh.

The team made ready for the outing to a village housing many of the coffee plantation workers.

All except Clair.

She sat on the cot bed in her tent, arms hugging her stomach and rocked backwards and forwards, moaning quietly to herself.

"Is there anything I can get you, Clair? Are you sure you don't want me to stay behind and look after you?"

Penny felt concerned. Her friend really seemed to be suffering badly with stomach cramps.

"No, I'll be fine," Clair answered, in-between a few groans. "I must've eaten something that didn't agree with me. I'll stay at the camp and rest up today. It will pass, I'm sure. You don't need to miss the trip, so go and enjoy yourself. Chris has given me tablets for the cramps, which will kick in soon. Off you go Penny, the others are waiting."

"Well, if you're sure Clair. We won't be long. Now take care of yourself," and Penny leant over and gave the nurse a hug.

Clair stood by the tent and waved as the land rovers trundled passed. She couldn't help noticing the smile on Chris's face as he turned his head to say something to Penny, who was sitting next to him.

Once I've finally finished with her, you will only feel revulsion, my darling. That smile is for me and only me. You will love me Chris and I'll do whatever it takes to make that happen.

Clair ducked back into her tent and quickly put on her walking boots and bush hat. She was excited. Her devious mind had gone into overdrive and with great anticipation she walked along the dirt road to the homestead.

The one storey, slate roofed wooden house, hemmed in by the veranda wending its way around the perimeter came into view.

Now to visit Angus McFadden and find out exactly why there's bad feeling between him and Chris and hope I can use it to destroy our precious Penny.

She hurried along the driveway and up the steps to the veranda where Molly was wielding a broom with gusto.

"Hullo Molly. Is Mr. McFadden home?"

Molly stopped sweeping and as she straightened up, hands on ample hips, stared at the nurse. She prided herself on being a good judge of character and had developed an instinctive dislike for this young lady yesterday. Seeing her so early this morning sent alarm bells ringing in her head but she leant her brush against the wall and said, "the master is still eating his breakfast. I will take you to him," and led the way into the house and along the passage to the homely kitchen. Gleaming copper pans dangled from hooks hanging over the wood fuelled stove. Wooden kitchen surfaces, bleached white from constant cleaning complimented the polished slate grey flagstones of the floor, bearing testimony to the pride Molly took in her cleaning duties. An aroma of freshly brewed coffee permeating the kitchen greeted the visitor.

Angus, seated at the wooden kitchen table brooding over a mug of coffee, looked up in surprise mixed with irritation.

"Nurse Clair to see you," Molly announced, and then abruptly turned and went back to her cleaning, leaving Clair standing in the door way, wondering if this was a good idea or not.

Molly doesn't like me, she surmised, as she smiled at Angus and apologised for disturbing him so early.

"I'm not sure what time the others will be back, so I took advantage of this opportunity to see you. I hope you don't mind."

Her voice trailed away into uncertainty whilst Angus looked steadily at her for a moment before speaking.

"Well, I didn't expect to see you quite so soon, but now you're here, would you like some coffee. There's a mug over there, and the coffee is on the stove."

"Thank you. I'd love some," and Clair helped herself before sitting down at the table, facing the plantation owner.

"I expect you're wondering why I asked to see you again." Clair hesitated, and then decided to come straight to the point. "Last night it was obvious you and Chris can't stand one another. Well, Penny has something that rightfully belongs to me and I'm determined to have it, and as you mentioned yesterday, you want justice, so I really think we could work well together to achieve both our ends."

"So, what has the delightful Nurse Penny got that you want so desperately," asked Angus, a sneer in his voice as he stared at the nurse.

Clair looked at him for a moment before answering.

"Doctor Chris Maynard."

"What! You want that lying bastard Maynard! Why?"

"He belongs to me, only me. Penny is in the way. I would've had Chris by now if it hadn't been for that two faced bitch. She said she wasn't interested. Go for it, Clair, she said. Doctor Maynard is all yours. I won't stand in your way." The nurse stopped talking, trembling with anger, coffee spilling out of her mug and onto the table.

Angus remained silent, his mind racing. What an interesting turn of events. Personally, he could see why Chris had fallen for Penny. Any right thinking man would. He'd noticed the doctor couldn't keep his eyes off the nurse. And just that knowledge alone inflamed his already red- hot rage against the man who'd killed his wife. How grossly unfair was this existence! How dare Maynard have a future to look forward to when his own stretched out into infinity, empty and alone; loneliness; unbearable loneliness his life long companion.

The idea of destroying the doctor with the help of this scheming female appealed to him immeasurably. Chris's life would be hell on earth saddled with this witch.

"Right Clair. What have you in mind?"

The nurse stared into her mug of coffee mentally plucking up courage before answering Angus McFadden's question.

"First of all I need to know what you've got against Chris that makes you hate him so much. Saying he killed your wife explains nothing. Penny is a sucker when it comes to sob stories, so although you probably think I'm being callous and insensitive, your story could be just what I need to manoeuvre Penny into a situation that will totally discredit our little nurse in the eyes of Chris. I couldn't care less what you think of him, Angus. I love him and will destroy anybody who tries to get in-between us. So, will you tell me what happened?"

The Scotsman emptied his pipe into an ashtray and refilled it with tobacco from a leather pouch. Oh yes, this was definitely a way of getting even. Anything he could do to get Chris saddled with this charming female would be worth it.

"Your Doctor Maynard killed my wife. O.K. He didn't put a gun to her head, or anything like that, but he killed her all the same, and left the boy motherless."

"The boy?" Clair was puzzled. There was no evidence of a child in the house.

"Yes, the boy. He doesn't live with me. I haven't seen him since the day he was born and my Lisa died." Angus fell silent, as memories of that day surfaced in his mind, and the anguish and hatred boiled up ready to consume him again.

He drew deeply on his pipe before continuing.

"My so-called friend Doctor Chris Maynard loved Lisa. Oh, he always denied it, but I know he did. Lisa said I was being silly, that Chris was only a good friend but I knew different. And I know that boy was the result of their union. Lisa always said she was expecting my baby, but I didn't believe her. Then Chris was supposedly ill and Lisa insisted on going to him even though I forbade her. She wanted me to go with her but I wouldn't, so she went anyway, and the rains came and she got stuck in the mud, and then a tree was hit by lightening and fell on the truck and my Lisa was trapped."

Angus couldn't continue. He remembered his wife's battered and broken body lying on a makeshift stretcher, carried by villagers who'd found her and brought her to the homestead. And then Chris Maynard arriving, looking as fit as a fiddle, his illness totally exaggerated by the bush telegraph. And then Lisa giving birth prematurely, labour brought on by the accident, Chris saving his child, but not Lisa. And what were his darling's last words?

"Don't blame Chris."

Well, he did blame Chris. He blamed him for Lisa being out that day and getting trapped, he blamed him for not saving her life but able to save the boy, he blamed him for making Lisa love him, but above all, Angus blamed himself for not being there when Lisa so desperately needed him, and having to live with that guilt day and night. And the only way he could live with it was to stoke the flames of hatred against Chris Maynard.

Angus stood up and looked out of the window, staring unseeingly at the rows of coffee bushes growing beyond his garden.

Clair stayed silent. Her imagination could easily fill in the pieces Angus wasn't able to talk about.

Now, how could she use this knowledge to drive an irreversible wedge between Penny and Chris?

The answer was obvious.

A simple plan culminating in devastating results for the poor little dove. Would the plantation owner play along? Clair had no doubt he would.

This is going to be so easy, she thought, and poured herself another mug of coffee.

"Can I top yours up, Angus? We have plans to discuss."

CHAPTER TWELVE

After spending the morning examining potential patients, it was time to call a halt for lunch.

Chris knew the whereabouts of a scenic reservoir not far from the village, an ideal place to eat and relax after a busy morning. Penny jumped at the chance to see more of this beautiful country although the nuns preferred to stay behind as a pregnant villager was in labour and needed their help. They'd assisted at many deliveries, so Chris was happy to leave them to it. Tribal culture also dictated no males allowed at the birth, so after leaving instructions with the nuns to send Joseph to the watering hole if complications developed, Chris was delighted to have his nurse to himself for once.

Penny stretched her arms above her head and breathed a deep sigh of contentment.

Multi coloured birds darted in and out of lush green foliage chasing flying insects, whilst red, gold and yellow butterflies accompanied sapphire tinted dragonflies flitting over the shimmering surface of the reservoir, wings iridescent in the sunlight. Baboons barked in the distance with answering calls of responding troops barely audible in the lazy heat. The constant muted buzzing of countless insects created the perfect back- drop to this magical world.

"This is absolutely beautiful," said Penny, leaning back against a rock as she admired the view across the water. "Look! There's zebra and wildebeest drinking on the far side. I'm not mistaken, am I?"

"No," said Chris, smiling at Penny's enthusiasm, "although the best time of day to see animals is in the evening, so we're lucky in having a group come now."

He lifted a bottle of orange juice from the cool box. "Let me give you a refill."

Watching Penny sip her drink, the doctor had an overwhelming urge to gather the nurse in his arms and say, "I love you."

But dare I do that, not knowing how the dove feels about me? he thought. I *know Penny likes me, but she has that reserve about her, a barrier, not wanting to get too close to people in case she gets hurt again. Damn the man that hurt her. I wonder if he's regretting what he did?*

"Is there anything wrong, Chris? You look stern, almost angry. I really am sorry about yesterday. I can't tell you how much I regret asking Angus about his wife."

Chris reached over and clasped Penny's hands.

He smiled and said, "don't be silly, Penny. You didn't do anything wrong. And no, I'm not angry. I wasn't even thinking about Angus. Shall we take a walk before going back to the village? There's a magnificent waterfall I'd like you to see not far from where we are."

"Really! Yes, I'd love to," said Penny and scrambled to her feet. "Lead the way."

The doctor clasped her hand as he helped the nurse negotiate several slippery rocks and then didn't let go. Penny thought of removing her hand, decided that would be churlish, so was content to leave it where it was, enjoying the feel of his gentle but firm grip.

The waterfall was spectacular.

Multiple rainbows shimmered in the cascading water, each droplet a precious stone radiating colour only to be dashed into tiny pieces as it hit the waiting river.

"Oh," gasped Penny. "This is so beautiful. Look at those colours."

Words failed her as she turned to the doctor, her exquisite eyes rivalling the beauty of the surrounding vista.

Chris was lost and all thoughts of taking things slowly deserted him as he reached for the nurse, pulled her into his arms and rained tender, feather soft kisses over her upturned face and neck, resting his mouth over the thudding pulse in her nape, hands smoothly moulding her body against his. His kisses slowly retraced their path up the side of her neck, before placing his mouth firmly but gently on her parted lips, and did what he'd been yearning to do for so long; kiss his love thoroughly, tasting the delights of her lips as she hesitantly and then with growing ardour responded to his love making. The surrounding scenery vanished to be replaced with mounting desire that threatened to engulf them. They were alone in the world, two souls locked in an embrace that united their physical senses into one cohesive longing for ultimate fulfilment. Kissing and caressing combined to captivate the lovers, igniting their bodies in one escalating flame that grew stronger with each loving caress, each feverish kiss...

They came to their senses simultaneously, moving abruptly away from each other.

Penny, trembling uncontrollably, stared at the doctor who was struggling to speak, his racing heart preventing any words being uttered. Her response had delighted and thrilled him, leaving him speechless.

She turned her face to the waterfall; drops of spray cooled her burning cheeks. She tried to make sense of what had happened. Each nerve ending in her body was quivering with desire, calling out for the ultimate fulfilment that had been denied them. Never had she felt passion like this before; the sensation of her body pressed against the doctor's, already permanently etched in her brain, the impression of his lips on hers still sending pulses of nerve tingling expectancy throughout her inner self. How her body longed for his.

Two strong hands rested gently on her shoulders and the nurse turned to face the person who had now completely and utterly turned her world upside down.

"Penny, my darling Penny. Please forgive me. I just couldn't help myself. You look so beautiful and I've wanted to kiss you from the very first time I saw you at the hospital in Colhaven. Take it slowly, I kept telling myself, take it slowly, but I just couldn't stop myself. Penny, I love you; I love you so very much. No, don't say anything." He put his finger against her lips. "I don't expect anything from you now. All I ask is you give me a chance to prove to you how much I love you, and will always love you. I've guessed you've been badly hurt in the pass. Penny, I will never hurt you but I realise you need time."

The nurse was silent, her thoughts and emotions in total confusion. The way her body and soul responded to the doctor's lovemaking had caught her completely off guard. The sensations still coursing through her body were alien. Never had she felt this way with Michael. Her feelings for her ex paled into total insignificance compared to what she was experiencing now. Was this true love, or just being caught up in the moment in this romantic place with a handsome doctor as her escort? Did Chris really mean the things he'd just said?

Doctor Maynard understood the confusion passing over her face.

"Yes, Penny. I do mean what I say. I love you with all my heart. I have never said that to another woman. I have never loved another woman. You, young lady, have turned this cynical doctor into an adoring love struck fool, who is now wishing he'd held on to his emotions a little while longer," and his voice trailed off into uncertainty.

Penny smiled shyly.

"I had no idea you felt that way about me Chris. I have feelings for you too but I was scared of them, scared to let go, scared of being hurt again. I vowed to myself before leaving England I didn't want to know a man romantically again. I didn't want to get involved, but the more I got to know you, I couldn't help my feelings for you develop. I tried so hard to ignore them, especially knowing Clair... oh my goodness, CLAIR!" Penny stopped in mid sentence, feelings of dismay and horror sweeping through her.

"Clair? What has Clair got to do with this," asked Doctor Maynard mystified, attempting to take Penny into his arms again, but failing as she placed her hands against his chest.

"I promised Clair," Penny paused, unsure how to continue.

"Promised her what?"

Penny stayed silent. How could she betray Clair like this? What was she thinking of! Clair loved Chris. She'd made no secret of that fact, and Clair was even at this moment back at camp feeling ill, too sick to come on this trip. And now Penny was betraying her. No, she couldn't do it.

She stepped away from the doctor, shaking her head.

"I'm so sorry Chris. This is a huge mistake. I'm so sorry," and before her resolve failed, she turned and hurried back along the path they'd taken to get to the waterfall.

Doctor Maynard stared at her retreating figure for a minute; hesitation etched on his face, then decision made, swiftly caught up with her. As he reached Penny, he gently took the nurse's arm and turned her to face him.

"Penny, don't worry my darling. I won't make a nuisance of myself, I promise you."

"It's not that, Chris, it's just, I'm sorry, I just can't tell you. Please forgive me."

I must do or say something to diffuse the situation, thought the doctor, *otherwise those barriers will go up and I might never breach them again.*

He reached for Penny's hand and gave it a squeeze.

"Hey, don't look so worried. Let's try and forget anything has happened, and carry on enjoying this lovely day. See that bright yellow bird over there? It's known as a weaverbird, so called because of the way it weaves its nest," and Chris deliberately kept the conversation on mundane topics, allowing Penny time to recover her composure. His tactics were rewarded with a smile and a funny anecdote on Penny's part about Ruth's baby, and by the time they reached the village, the familiar feeling of comradeship was back and Penny was able to admire the newborn with outward composure.

The trip back to camp passed all too quickly and they were met by Clair who was feeling much better thank you, the tablets and a good rest was all she'd needed to feel as right as rain again.

"Did you have a good time Penny?" asked Clair, following the nurse to her tent.

"Yes, I did," she replied, and then felt the tell tell blush creep up her neck and into her face.

I hope Clair didn't notice, thought Penny, as she busied herself organising her sleeping bag. *I hate feeling guilty like this.*

Clair had noticed.

She sat on the cot in her tent, brooding over the day's events.

You've been getting your claws into my doctor. Boy, I can see right into your scheming little brain because you are so transparent, Penny Whickam. And Chris is falling for your holier than thou attitude. Right! I can see I'll have to move quicker than I thought. Angus has given me plenty to work with. You are going to burn lady, and her thoughts returned to the morning and her very constructive chat with Angus McFadden.

Poor Penny. Little do you know what's in store for you. That smile will be wiped off your face so fast you won't know what's hit you. You think you've got Chris wrapped around your little finger? Well, you are so wrong, you scheming little witch. He's mine, all mine.

CHAPTER THIRTEEN

Molly was in the kitchen preparing dinner for Angus plus three guests, Doctor Maynard, Nurse Penny and Nurse Clair.

She still couldn't believe it! The boss had actually invited his sworn enemy to his home!

What a turn around, she thought, as nimble fingers busily chopped onions, carrots and sweet potatoes for a casserole she was preparing for the evening.

Not a kind word has been spoken about the doctor since that terrible day when the beautiful Mrs. Lisa died, and the baby bundled off to Jinja. Boss Angus has hated him ever since and any suggestion to go to Jinja to see the baby met with shouting and cursing.

A tender expression crossed her face as she thought of the baby boy. Little did Angus know how often Molly visited him at his foster parents home.

He is so beautiful, just like his mother, but he has his father's temper and red hair. Molly shook her head sadly. *Would the boss ever forgive Doctor Chris? Who knows, this dinner party may be the start of better times to come. So, Molly, stop thinking and start doing. The guests will arrive soon, and you haven't even started dessert yet*, and she resumed preparing the vegetables, the sound of the chopping knife on the wooden board reaching fever pitch.

Back at camp, the doctor remained mystified at the invitation that came from Angus inviting the party for dinner.

Penny was delighted.

"This could be such a wonderful opportunity for you and Angus to bury your differences. Please say you'll go with an open mind, and if Angus holds out his hand in friendship, take it."

"Oh, I'll certainly do that. I'm just surprised, that's all. I wonder what Clair said to Angus for him to offer this invite?"

"Well, whatever it was, good for her, I say," and Penny smiled at her friend, who had joined the other two around the campfire.

"What did you say to Angus when he came to the camp this morning?"

"Nothing much. I just offered him a mug of coffee, and thanked him for returning my watch. I knew the clasp was faulty so I was lucky it fell off near the veranda when I hurried out to the land rover the other evening. So, the stomach cramps were a blessing in disguise. We talked a bit and he seemed genuinely sorry for the unfriendly reception he gave you Chris, so when I suggested this get together he jumped at the chance to make amends."

Clair walked over to the doctor and said, "I'm so glad I could arrange this for you. It would be wonderful if the two of you became friends again," and she smiled at him before turning to Penny.

"Angus asked if we could be at the homestead at around seven, as dinner will be ready for seven-thirty, so, time to put our glad rags on, or rather, a clean pair of jeans and t-shirt. I didn't bring any clothes suitable for a dinner party. Did you Penny?"

"No, I didn't. Roughing it was the order of the day so I was told," and she laughed as she went to her tent to wash off the days dust and change into clean bush clothes.

Six forty-five saw them in the land rover, bouncing along the dirt road, Clair in the front with the doctor, Penny sitting behind as usual.

She didn't mind as she had a lot to think about. Chris's declaration of love had certainly taken her by surprise, and her response to his lovemaking had stunned her.

Did she love Chris? She had to admit she did. She realised now she had fallen in love with him slowly but surely as they spent more time together, but had subconsciously kept her feelings under wraps, refusing to acknowledge them because of Clair. But to get over

Michael so soon? Was she that fickle? When she saw her fiancé kissing her best friend, she believed her world had come to an end. But now, it was almost as though she'd never had a relationship with him. That was how much it paled into insignificance compared to the feelings generated by the doctor.

Penny realised she felt sympathy for Michael and Jane. How difficult it must've been for them, the same difficulty she was feeling regarding Clair.

The nurse studied the back of Chris's well shaped head, aching to twine his thick, blond, sun bleached hair around her fingers. She wanted to kiss the nape of his neck and feel his arms around her again and hear his expressions of love in her ear. She yearned to tell the whole world she loved Doctor Chris Maynard with every ounce of her being, but knew this was not the right time, as her feelings of love became overshadowed by deep pangs of guilt every time she looked at Clair. It was obvious her friend thought the world of Chris, and to have managed to get an invite from Angus clearly delighted Clair for Chris's sake.

What a mess, Penny thought, and looked at the nurse smiling at the doctor whilst he was talking.

I know I'm going to have to tell her sooner or later. Oh, I hope she won't hate me. But I can't tell her yet, not whilst we're still on this trip. That won't be fair. I'll wait until we get back to The Haven. Then I'll tell her I love Chris and he loves me, and I'm so sorry as I didn't mean it to happen, but fate had other plans.

Chris glanced in the rear view mirror and was disturbed to see the worried expression on Penny's face.

Damn it! he thought. *I went too far today, telling Penny I love her. She's obviously thinking about what happened and the memories aren't pleasing her very much. I must put her mind at rest. I don't want this to affect our relationship at all, not until she's ready, because, my darling Penny, I love you too much*, and he smiled at the same time Penny looked up and met his eyes in the mirror.

Her heart raced as she saw the love in them, and she smiled back hoping he would see what she felt.

He did. There was no mistaking the message for him in those beautiful radiant eyes. Chris thought his heart was going to jump out of his chest, and it was all he could do not to slam on brakes, stop the vehicle and sweep Penny off the back seat and into his arms.

"Chris, did you hear what I said? Chris?" Clair's strident voice brought him back to reality.

"I'm sorry Clair. No, what did you say? My mind wandered just then."

"It doesn't matter. Anyway, there are the lights of the homestead. I wonder what Molly's cooked for us? I'm starving. Those tablets you gave me this morning worked wonders."

Although Clair was chatting away, she hadn't missed the look shared between Chris and Penny and bitter jealousy rose up like bile at the back of her throat threatening to choke her.

Angus must play his part well, she schemed, as they walked up the wooden steps to the veranda, to be greeted by their host, resplendent in a kilt of the McFadden tartan.

"Well," said Chris, holding out his hand to his old friend, "you have put me to shame, dressed like that. Thank you for this invite Angus. This means a lot to me."

"Got to let bygones be bygones, Chris. Time I moved on," and Angus turned his attention to the two nurses.

"Welcome ladies. I hope you'll enjoy your dinner. Molly's renowned for her cooking and it's a long time since she's put her skills to good use. I'm not really one for entertaining, so excuse a host who's a bit out of practice," and he ushered them into the house and to the lounge.

It was a masculine room, devoid of any feminine influence, with hunting trophies and menacing wooden African masks adorning the white washed walls, carved wooden elephants and giraffes gracing the bookcases. Several large zebra skins covered the stone flags. Illumination was from oil lamps, light flickering off the masks causing eyes and mouths to move grotesquely.

Penny shivered.

No photos of Lisa were on display, no evidence at all of her ever existing. Angus had tried to erase her from his life, succeeding outwardly, but deep inside she still existed.

Angus spoke, playing the attentive host.

"Would you like a drink before dinner, maybe a glass of sherry? Chris, I've beer in the fridge. Go and help yourself, you know where it is. Get me one as well, please. Meanwhile I'll pour the ladies a little aperitif."

The doctor walked along the passage to the kitchen, and saw Molly putting the finishing touches to dinner.

She beamed at him as he walked through the doorway.

"Oh, Doctor Chris! This is so wonderful. I never thought the master would do anything like this again. I remember the parties when Mrs. Lisa was alive. Everyone so happy then, always laughing and joking. But this past year..." her voice trailed away.

"I know, Molly. It's been a terrible time for you as well, I realise that. You remained loyal to Angus and I admire you tremendously for staying with him. I'm sure he hasn't been easy to live with, so let's hope he's finally ready to face life again. But let's take things as they come. I've just popped in to get a couple of beers. Your cooking smells great. You obviously haven't lost your touch," and he grinned at her as he cracked open the beers.

Meanwhile Angus had selected a sweet sherry for the nurses.

Mindful of Clair's instructions, he engaged Penny in small talk. When Angus McFadden put his mind to it, he could be a charming host, and Penny felt herself warm to this man who had suffered such a tragic loss in his life.

They were talking together when Chris returned from the kitchen. He offered a beer to Angus and then stood by Clair who was staring at one of the carved masks. She turned to the doctor.

"Don't you think Penny's getting on well with Angus? He really seems keen, and has obviously forgiven her for the faux pas she committed the other night. Oh Chris, it's great seeing him chatting away like this. Penny has such a knack for putting people at their ease. I so hope this evening will be a huge success."

Before the doctor could respond, Molly announced dinner was ready and please to take their places in the dining room.

She had pulled out all the stops.

This was a room Penny could admire.

The large oak table looked magnificent adorned with solid silver cutlery including silver napkin rings encasing crisp, white linen napkins edged with fine lace. Delicate china tableware complimented place settings decked with crystal glasses waiting in expectation for a variety of wines Angus had unearthed from his cellar. A stunning centrepiece of exotic purple and orange blooms of the Crane flower, better known as the Bird of Paradise stood proud in a tall intricately engraved crystal vase completing the splendour. They took their places on carved oak chairs cushioned in deep crimson velvet. Penny found it difficult to remember they were still in the middle of the bush!

"You have done me proud, Molly, and I know your cooking will be as good," and Angus smiled at his house girl, who beamed with pleasure before bustling away to dish up the first course of pumpkin soup drizzled with fresh cream followed by lamb casserole served with a variety of vegetables. A dessert of homemade vanilla ice cream made from clotted cream covered in a chocolate and mint sauce caused exclamations of delight from the guests. Finally, Molly brought in a platter of cheeses to go with savoury biscuits, and a large coffee pot of freshly ground coffee, product of the plantation.

"That was one of the most delicious meals I have ever eaten," said Penny, and held out her cup for a refill. "That lamb was delicious, so tender. I would love to have the recipe."

"Of course, Nurse Penny."

Molly was pleased. The meal had gone well, and her master had actually laughed, not once but several times. She noticed he'd enjoyed talking to Nurse Penny during the meal. Nurse Clair didn't seem to mind.

I believe Nurse Clair likes our doctor a lot, Molly thought, as she prepared to wash up the pots and pans. *I don't think that's such a good thing. Still, Doctor Chris is sensible. I'm sure he sees her for what she is,* and Molly dismissed them from her thoughts and concentrated on getting her kitchen back to its usual spotless condition.

The host and his guests were sitting on the veranda, nursing their coffee, a full moon negating the need for artificial light.

Talk was desultory, full stomachs having a mute affect on conversation.

Angus filled his pipe with tobacco from his leather pouch and looked at Chris.

"Did you find any patients amongst my workers, Chris? I haven't had any reports from Lucas, my boss boy. I'm sure he would've told me if there had been."

"No, Angus. We checked out the whole village and gave them a clean bill of health. I believe education is definitely the key, as the villagers were aware of what to expect with leprosy and have obviously been safeguarding themselves. So, that's good news."

Chris observed Angus through the haze of smoke drifting from his friend's pipe.

"Your coffee plants look healthy. Do you expect a good crop this year?"

"God willing. The seasons have been right for coffee growing. I heard you're supervising an extension to the clinic. How's that coming along?"

"Not bad. I've had problems with the suppliers but hopefully, once this trip is over, we should get back on track," and Chris began explaining the reasons for the delay in the building.

Clair turned to Penny and whispered, "shall we leave the men to it, and take a turn around the garden? I could do with some fresh air after all that food. My eyes just want to close, now that my stomach's full." She chuckled. "I feel like a baby that's just been fed."

"Good idea. I don't think we'll be missed for a while," and the girls walked down the veranda steps to the garden.

Although it was dark, there was enough illumination from the moon to clearly see ones way, so Clair suggested walking across the lawn to a large Jacaranda tree towering over a set of garden chairs nestled underneath.

"Actually Penny, there's something I want to discuss with you," said Clair, as she settled herself into one of the chairs.

Penny stiffened. Had Clair guessed her feelings for Chris?

"What about?"

"I heard some news I thought you might find interesting. Lisa, Angus's wife, died in childbirth, but the baby survived."

Shock and dismay swept through Penny.

"Oh Clair, how awful! I had no idea, and you say the baby survived?"

"Yes. Foster parents in Jinja look after him. And this is the really sad bit. Angus was so distraught at losing his wife he blamed Chris for not saving her, and he hasn't seen the baby since she died. It's almost as though he's also blaming the child for causing Lisa's death."

"Oh, that's so sad. Poor baby, to lose mum and dad at the same time. And you're certain Angus has no contact with him?"

"Apparently not." Clair waited a moment before continuing. "Wouldn't it be wonderful if somehow Angus could be persuaded to see his child? Maybe he'll change his mind and become a father to the boy."

Penny was silent, digesting this surprising news. What a waste of a year of a baby's life. How could he act this way? But surely there must be more to it than Angus blaming the baby and Chris for his wife's death?

"What do you say, Penny? Do you think you could persuade Angus to see his son?"

"Me! But I hardly know the man. I don't think he'll take kindly to me telling him what to do."

"I know it won't be easy, but he seems to enjoy talking to you. Maybe there'll be an opportunity you could take advantage of. Anyway, it's just a suggestion."

Clair sniffed the night air as the strong perfume of frangipani blossom wafted across the lawn. "Shall we go back and join the men? I'm wide awake now and I could drink another cup of that delicious coffee," and Clair stood up, stretched and ambled back across the lawn, pleased with herself, a sly grin playing around her mouth.

Our kind hearted Penny will be thinking over what I've just said. She's bound to want to help. After all, she is the dove, and our dove has a reputation to maintain.

Penny followed slowly, her tender heart awash with conflicting emotions.

Imagine bringing father and son together. But how to do that? Angus is a proud man. I'm not sure how he would feel about me interfering in his business, but having a son, and not having any contact with him, that's not right. I'm sure Lisa would be devastated if she knew. Somehow I must do something about this, get Angus and his son together. I wonder whereabouts in Jinja the foster parents are living? Maybe I could get a lift with Chris the next time he goes to town and see if I can find the baby.

Penny reached the top of the veranda steps.

Chris looked at his love, and felt concern over the frown clouding her beautiful face.

"Are you feeling O.K. Penny?" he asked, walking over to her. "You look worried about something."

"I'm fine, Chris, thanks. Just a little tired maybe."

"It's time we went back to camp anyway."

Chris turned to his host who was talking quietly with Clair.

"Time for us to make tracks, Angus. Thank you for this evening. I hope we'll be able to do it again, maybe on our way back from this trip?"

"Of course," said Angus, holding out his hand. "Just let me know when you're in the area." He turned to Penny and gave her a hug, which surprised her, as well as the doctor. "I've really enjoyed talking to you, Penny. I'll look forward to seeing you again soon. You to Clair."

Clair smiled at Angus, and nodded. Her plan was maturing nicely.

Chapter Fourteen

Six days later the expedition arrived back at The Haven.

The trip itself had been a success, especially in the educational field, and the team had located half a dozen villagers with the first signs of leprosy, eminently treatable with a good chance of no lasting deformities.

However, success or failure on the subject of relationships was questionable.

During the days and evenings of close proximity with the doctor, had Penny verbally declared her love to him? Were they able to spend time together participating in the activities lovers all over the world enjoy?

The answer, frankly, was no.

Why? Because Clair stuck to Chris like a leach, and not wanting to create bad feelings in the camp, Penny left things as they were. But, to be fair, Clair wasn't the only reason. Penny had been talking to Angus and what she'd learnt disturbed her.

And Doctor Maynard?

How he longed to hold Penny, kiss her, caress her and whisper those sweet nothings in her shell like ears, but there was Clair, always Clair.

However, was he being fair to the other nurse?

Penny didn't exactly try to be alone with him. And there were those little asides from Clair, about how well Penny had bonded with Angus, how the Scotsman enjoyed talking to her. Certainly on that last evening they spent at the coffee plantation on their way back to the Haven, Angus monopolized his dove.

Chris thought about that visit. Penny didn't seem to mind. In fact, whilst listening to Angus, she had such a look of empathy on her face it surprised the doctor.

Chris Maynard walked away from his desk to look out of the window.

The sun was low in the sky, casting pink and gold hues over the foliage in the garden, firing up the bougainvillea, creating a stunning setting, but the doctor didn't see it. All he saw was the sympathetic look on Penny's face as she listened to Angus.

Don't be stupid. Penny is a compassionate person. That's one of the reasons she's so special. I certainly don't blame Angus for opening his heart to my love. Not even a huge iceberg would be impervious to her charms.

Chris had to smile.

If I didn't know you better, Doctor Chris Maynard, I would say you were feeling just a few pangs of jealousy. So, don't be ridiculous. You'll see Penny at dinner tonight, and come hell or high water, you'll take her for a romantic stroll around the garden, without the insidious Clair, and see what ensues.

This action decided, Chris went back to his desk and buried himself in his paper work.

Meanwhile, his love had her own problems to think about.

Penny was back on the ward, helping Sister Mercy with the dressings, her nimble fingers applying soothing ointments and fresh bandages to those patients who had fingers and toes eaten away by the disease.

Her mind was replaying the last conversation she'd had with Angus.

He'd told her the baby's father was Chris!

She couldn't, wouldn't believe it.

But Angus remained adamant. And that's why he wasn't interested in the child. Chris was the father, and he knew it. If he had any guts, he would admit it and take responsibility for his son.

Uncertainty reigned high in Penny's mind. She realised to find out the truth she needed to visit Jinja and see for herself. She believed she knew Chris well enough to know he would accept responsibility if the baby was his. The fact that he hadn't, made her even more determined to get to the truth, because if Angus was mistaken, how tragic for him to remain so lonely when he had a son to love.

After dinner, Chris asked Penny to accompany him on a stroll around the garden. "I haven't had a minute alone with you for nearly a week, so, will you accept my invite?"

"Of course I will," said Penny. "It's such a beautiful evening, a leisurely walk will be perfect."

The moon, although losing its fullness, still cast a silvery glow over the grounds, mysterious shadows appearing and disappearing as clouds scuttled across the moon's surface. Bats flew overhead, as the couple made their way to the alcove opposite the doctor's office.

"Better make sure there's no green mambas slithering around," said Chris, leading the nurse to the seat.

"Even thinking about that evening brings me out in a cold sweat. Thank goodness you noticed the snake before it could strike. I wouldn't be sitting here on this beautiful evening otherwise," and Penny shivered at the memory.

"Well, you are here and I couldn't be more happy. Penny, I meant what I said at the waterfall, and, I know I promised I wasn't going to say anything, but, the way you responded to my kissing you and the few words you whispered; is there any possibility you have feelings for me?"

"Oh Chris, of course I do! Yes, I was taken totally by surprise when you told me you loved me." She hesitated a little before continuing, shyness causing her voice to drop to a murmur. "I was amazed at the way I responded when you kissed me, because I'd never felt that way before even though I was due to get married before this Uganda trip came up."

Penny lowered her head; her chestnut curls tumbling around her face.

"My fiancé and best friend had fallen in love and they didn't know how to tell me. I saw them kissing one day and broke off the engagement, so when I bumped into you and you told me about this country and the work you were doing, I just knew it was fate working, and I had to come. But the last thing I expected or wanted was to fall in love. I was determined to keep men out of my life in that respect. But," she lifted her head and smiled her gentle, loving smile at the doctor, "I hadn't counted on a certain Doctor Chris Maynard showing me what true love really is."

Chris's self control could no longer be restrained.

He swept Penny into his arms and kissed her single-mindedly, savouring the softness of her lips, tasting the delights of her open mouth as she pressed herself close to him, the sheer maleness of him overpowering her senses until the nurse felt she was going to literally melt in his arms as waves of passion swept over her.

Then feelings of guilt took over.

Clair, always Clair rising like a spectre between them.

With a sound that was almost a groan, Penny gently pulled herself out of the doctor's arms. Chris released her immediately.

"What's wrong my love? I haven't hurt you, have I?"

"No, Chris. I'm sorry; this isn't the right time. I can't explain just yet. Please be patient with me. There's something I have to do first." She put her hand to the doctor's cheek and gently stroked his face. "Just give me a little time, please."

"I'll try, Penny," answered Chris, "Just tell me what it is you have to do."

"I can't just yet, but I will, I promise you. Please trust me to do the right thing."

Penny was distraught to see the bewilderment in her doctor's eyes, but she knew she had to tell Clair about her feelings for Chris before the nurse found out from other sources. She'd been a coward, putting the moment off, but no longer. She didn't want her friend humiliated like she'd been with Michael and Jane. No, at the first opportunity she would tell Clair outright and hope she would understand. Yes, she'll be upset and probably hate Penny for a while, but hopefully, after time, Clair would understand and forgive her.

Now it was Chris's turn to be worried. He saw conflicting emotions cross Penny's face and immediately thought of Angus.

Don't be stupid. Angus has no bearing on Penny's thoughts. Respect her privacy, and when the time is right, I'll declare my love for my darling to the world when I make her my wife, and he smiled reassuringly before leading her away from the alcove and back to the main building.

Once Penny and the doctor disappeared from view, Clair slowly eased her way out from behind two closely growing bushes.

She'd eavesdropped on the two lovers.

Her feelings for Chris remained unchanged. He was under the influence of a lying, scheming witch and couldn't be blamed for believing he was in love with her. Clair wasn't worried. Once she exposed Penny's true nature to Chris, he'll turn to her for comfort, and she'll be waiting, her arms wide open to receive him and love him the way only she could do.

After all, she was Chris's one true love.

CHAPTER FIFTEEN

More trouble loomed with the non -delivery of building supplies.

"It looks like another trip to Jinja," lamented Chris the next morning. "This whole extension is turning into a nightmare."

Penny realised Chris's misfortune could be her opportunity to find out more about the baby.

"It's my day off today. Would you like some company?"

Of course, the doctor was delighted.

"Absolutely, Penny. Can you be ready for ten? The journey will take about an hour, and once I've completed what I have to do, I'll take you sight seeing."

At ten on the dot, Penny, dressed in emerald green slacks and shirt highlighting the chestnut tints in her hair, stood waiting for the doctor outside her quarters,

My dove is looking beautiful, thought Chris, as he pulled up in the land rover.

"Hop on board, Penny. I persuaded cook to pack a picnic basket for us. Shall we have lunch at the Owen Falls Dam? The view is quite spectacular. Have you brought your camera?"

Penny nodded, feeling unexpectedly shy in the presence of the overpowering masculinity exuding from this man she adored.

Soon they were heading for the tarmac road leading to Jinja.

The usual sellers lined the way surrounded by luscious mangoes and the large fruit of the baobab tree, containing cream of tartar, the white pulp surrounding the seeds. Now and again, chimps and baboons ran across the road, and they slowed down once, allowing a herd of buck to amble across, amazingly unfazed by the motor.

Penny loved it all. She had an enduring smile on her face as she surveyed her surroundings, wishing her parents could experience all this for themselves.

She turned to Chris, eyes glowing radiantly, and gave him such a dazzling smile his heart raced. He reached out a hand and gently clasped one of hers.

"You look as though you're enjoying yourself. Uganda is a wonderful country, isn't it?"

"I'm loving it. There's something about Africa that gets under your skin. I know I've only been here a short time, but I'm amazed at how much I feel at home. I'll be sorry to leave when the time comes."

"Well, who knows what the future holds. You may stay longer than you thought. Ah, here's the Jinja turn off. It's nice to see the Indian population returning. They are amazing at creating businesses and that's exactly what Uganda needs to get back on her feet. That plus investment from other countries of course."

They drove along wide dusty streets flanked by old style colonial buildings in various states of repair. It was obvious that the town had been through a tough time but entrepreneurial townsmen and women were intent on rebuilding the prosperity Jinja enjoyed before the ruinous regime of Idi Amin. Hindu temples dominated the sky-line and Penny was fascinated to see a much- loved bronze statue of Mahatma Gandhi who had held a special affection for this African town, which was reciprocated by the inhabitants. Popular restaurants, their painted facades decorated in extravagant colours drew in the crowds intent on sampling a variety of menus, Indian cuisine being high on the list.

Chris pulled up outside an hotel.

"Do you fancy a cool drink? My friend Rivas runs this hotel and does a mean mango and pineapple mix that is guaranteed to put a spring in your step, and no, there's no alcohol involved. The secret ingredient is some concoction he imports from India, but that's all he'll tell me. Would you like to try some?"

"Sounds wonderful," and Penny was out of her seat before the doctor turned off the engine.

She was enchanted.

The hotel, built in the old colonial style with a large veranda circling the building, was painted brilliant white, whilst the shutters and ironwork contrasted vividly in peacock blue, the same colour as the sky. Hotel staff, dressed in traditional Indian costumes, glided quietly pass, seeing to the needs of the guests.

"Indian women are beautiful, don't you think? Look at the young lady over there wearing the amazing pink sari trimmed with gold. She is striking!"

No more beautiful than you, thought Chris, but mindful of what Penny had said the previous evening, kept quiet.

They drank exotic fruit juice out of tall crystal glasses, seated by a marble fountain, the water flowing out of the beak of a magnificent white marble swan, wings outstretched, neck extended looking heavenward ready to take flight.

"What a stunning sculpture," exclaimed Penny. "In fact, this whole hotel is stunning. Your friend has done a grand job."

"It was pretty derelict when he returned to Jinja. He was a young child when he fled the country with his parents who owned the building. During Amin's dictatorship, the hotel was looted, and all valuables taken by Amin's savage soldiers. Now though, Rivas has been able to bring The Flying Swan Hotel back to its former beauty. It has Michelin stars, which puts it on the map for tourists. Spread the word to your parents. Maybe they'd like to come to Uganda for a holiday, see their lovely daughter and stay in this outstanding hotel."

"It's funny you should say that. I was thinking about them on the way. I know they would both love it. Who knows! I'd love to see them and put my mother's mind at rest at the same time. I want to show her how happy I am living and working in this beautiful country."

Chris looked at his watch.

"Time for my first appointment, unfortunately. Are you sure you'll be O.K. for a couple of hours, Penny?"

She nodded. "I'll be fine, Chris. I'm looking forward to wandering around for a bit. We'll stick to our arrangement and I'll meet you back here at one. I saw a few interesting buildings I'd like to explore. Don't worry. I won't wander off the beaten track, I promise."

Chris bent down and brushed a fleeting kiss on Penny's cheek.

"Don't forget, be here at one or I'll send a search party out for you."

She smiled at his retreating form, and then her face turned serious.

Right, Penny. Where to start? You don't have much to go on. Angus said he doesn't know who the foster parents are, although Clair was under the impression friends of Chris took the baby in. If I find the building where births and deaths are registered, I might learn something.

Penny went to the receptionist and asked where births were registered.

The receptionist was helpful and gave directions to the town hall.

"You can't miss it. The building has a tall clock tower on the right hand side and a large expanse of lawn in the front. It will take you about ten minutes to walk."

"Thank you so much," said Penny, and soon she was striding along the pavement towards the town hall.

Jinja's a bustling town and Penny felt her excitement rising as she skirted street vendors selling intricately hand woven baskets of varying sizes, colourful bead work with geometric designs as well as wooden sculptors depicting typical scenes of African life.

Look at that carving of a lion, it looks so life like. And that elephant! Oh, and those painted carvings of African women carrying urns of water on their heads are amazing, she thought, mindful of the fact she had work to do but longing to spend time examining all these wonderful offerings laid out before her.

I must make a plan to come back and just browse. There's so much to see, but I don't have time now. And anyway, there's the town hall.

She stood in front of an imposing building, also built on colonial lines with wide steps leading to large wooden double doors, brass handles gleaming in the sun.

Once inside, the temperature plummeted and Penny shivered, feeling the full force of the air conditioning.

She walked towards a wooden counter screened by glass and waited in line to be served. The clerk oozed efficiency, and within five minutes Penny was asking if she had records of a white baby born a year ago and fostered by a couple living in Jinja.

"All such records are confidential, madam. Are you a relative?"

"No, just a friend. But it's really important I find out the whereabouts of this child. His father's happiness is at stake. Couldn't you bend the rules just a little?"

"I am sorry, but no. Until I get official authorisation from the foster parents, I'm not allowed to divulge any information. Come back, madam, when you have the authorisation. Next please!"

Penny wasn't surprised. This had been a long shot, but even so, she felt disappointed.

"Now what?" she said aloud, and stood at the top of the steps surveying the bustling scene before her, hoping for some inspiration.

"There must be another way of finding out where this baby is living. Someone must know. But who?"

Whilst Penny stood looking at the throng of people walking pass the steps she suddenly realised she recognised one particular person.

"Goodness! That's Molly, Angus's house girl. I wonder what she's doing in Jinja?"

Penny raced down the steps to catch up with the employee, who had disappeared down a side street. "Molly would know," and hurried after the woman, who'd stopped at a gate opening onto a garden path leading to a two-storey house.

As Molly fumbled with the latch, Penny caught up with her.

"Hullo, Molly."

Molly turned and then beamed at the nurse.

"If it isn't Nurse Penny! This is a surprise. How nice to see you. But you are here alone in Jinja?"

"No, Molly. I came with Doctor Chris. He's busy at the moment, and actually, I'm pleased I've bumped into you because I think you might be able to help me with a problem."

"A problem? Nurse Penny has a problem?"

Penny nodded. "Molly, do you have time to have a cup of coffee with me? There's something I need to discuss with you. It won't take long, I promise."

The house girl looked intently at the nurse.

Shame, Nurse Penny looks really worried. Well, she is a very nice lady. Let me see if I can help her with her problem.

Molly nodded. "There's a coffee shop at the end of this road. We can sit there and you can tell me why you look so troubled."

Sitting opposite Molly, two steaming cups of coffee in front of them, Penny told the maid what she knew about the baby boy.

"I realise it's none of my business, Molly, but it seems so sad Angus could have a son and because of his pride or whatever, deprive himself of being a father and that little boy, his rightful parent. I really want to find out the truth, not just for Angus's sake, but also for mine and I so hope you'll be able to help me."

Penny stopped talking and waited for Molly to reply.

"Well, Nurse Penny, you are the answer to my prayers. For a year now I have visited that little baby, watching him grow more and more like his father. But whenever I tried to speak to Boss Angus about the boy, oh dear, he either shouted at me or just walked away. Now I say nothing. Boss Angus doesn't know I visit his son on my days off. He said I must have nothing to do with him. But I loved Madam Lisa very much, and I made a promise when she died that I would watch over her son. I do not understand how Boss Angus could think the baby is Doctor Chris's! Grief at losing his wife made his mind not think straight. How he hates the doctor," and Molly took a large gulp of coffee as though to swallow her anger at her boss.

"But I thought they'd become friends again, Molly?"

"Well, I hope so, Nurse Penny." The house girl sounded doubtful.

There was silence for a while, and then Molly spoke.

"Nurse Penny, do you want to see the boy? If you see him I am sure you will know that Boss Angus is the father. Maybe the boss will listen to you. I believe he has a lot of respect for you."

"Yes, Molly. I would love to see the baby. Is that where you were going when I caught up with you?"

"Yes. He lives with friends of Doctor Chris's. The husband owns the Flying Swan Hotel."

"Rivas!"

"Yes, Nurse Penny. Have you met him?"

"No, but Doctor Chris took me to the hotel earlier when we arrived in Jinja. What an amazing place. The sculptured swan is wonderful."

"They are a lovely couple and although they've five children of their own, they have treated the baby as though he were their own child. But I know they would want him to be with his father. Madam Rivas has encouraged me to speak to Boss Angus whenever I could hoping he would be willing to see the child." Molly shook her head sadly. "So far, Boss Angus has always refused." She smiled broadly at Penny. "But now, Miss Penny, he may listen to you. I know he likes you very much. If you ask him he might change his mind."

"Well, let's see what happens. Can I come with you to see the baby now? Do you think Madam Rivas would mind?"

"She will be very happy."

Penny looked at her watch. "I've an hour before I need to be back at the hotel, so yes, let's go."

They retraced their steps to the gate, and soon were walking along the garden path to a house surrounded by jacaranda and flamboyant trees. Brilliantly coloured flowers jostled for space in the flowerbeds, bees hovering over them, spoilt for choice.

The house, painted in pale rose pink, felt warm and inviting.

Walking up the stone steps to the veranda, Penny knew peace and tranquillity were the keywords describing this home.

Chris couldn't have picked better, she thought, as Molly knocked on the door.

A short pause, and then the door was opened by the mistress of the house who greeted Molly with a hug and a kiss on both cheeks.

"Lovely to see you again, Molly."

Turning to Penny she asked, "And who is this? Let me guess. One of the nurses working at The Haven?"

The smiling face of an exquisite Indian lady, dressed in an apricot coloured sari threaded with gold looked enquiringly at Penny, who smiled back, nodding in agreement.

"Madame Rivas, this is Nurse Penny, the dove as she is known at The Haven. I have spoken about her before."

"Of course! Welcome Penny. It's very nice to meet you. Molly has told me of you. You were very complimentary about her cooking."

Penny smiled at the mistress of the house. "Molly's cooking is delicious. I'm sure I put on at least six pounds at my last visit."

Madam Rivas led the way to the lounge.

"What a beautiful home you have," exclaimed Penny, her eyes delighting in the mixture of old and new, Indian and European that made up the furniture and fixtures of the room.

"You have an eye for decorating. Everything so different but mixing so well together."

Madam Rivas smiled her pleasure. She was justly proud of her home and had spent a lot of time and thought on the decoration. To have this delightful young nurse complimenting her was an added bonus.

"Please take a seat. What refreshment would you like? Tea, coffee or fruit juice?"

"Fruit juice please," answered Penny.

"And you, Molly?"

"Fruit juice would be fine, Madam Rivas."

After giving instructions to the waiting maid, Madam Rivas sat back in her chair and spoke to Molly.

"Little Angus is not so little anymore," she said, laughing. "He's just waking from his nap, so Rosina will bring him from the nursery. He loves having you visit him. Does Nurse Penny know about the baby?"

"Yes she does, Madam Rivas. That is why she is here today."

Madam Rivas looked at Penny, who said, "I really would like to help. When I heard the story of this little boy I felt so frustrated, knowing how lonely Angus is, but how stubborn and pig headed he's being. I can't believe the baby is Doctor Chris's and I'm hoping to persuade Angus to see his son."

Rosina arrived with a tray of glasses, and after distributing the refreshments, went to the nursery to collect the baby.

"But he's a carbon copy of Angus," exclaimed Penny, as Molly held out her arms to the child, who gurgled in excitement and wriggled out of Rosina's arms to be with his friend. "Even down to his hair. Angus has copper curls, and his beard also has a red tinge to it. No, there's no mistaking who's the father," and Penny smiled delightedly at the baby jumping up and down on Molly's legs as she balanced him holding his arms. "To think Angus has never seen his son. Oh, how he will kick himself for not believing Chris. But, it's not too late."

Penny turned to Madam Rivas, who was fondly watching the child.

"Madam Rivas, I realise you love little Angus, having looked after him from birth. How would you feel if I could persuade his father to visit? Would you mind very much? Would you be willing to let the baby be with his father?"

"Penny, the baby should be with his proper father. When Chris asked us to look after him when his mother died, we thought it would be for a short time, time enough for Angus to recover a little from his wife's death. We knew Molly would be perfectly able to look after the baby but then Angus wouldn't have anything to do with the child. When I heard he thought the baby was Chris's I couldn't believe my ears! But Angus is, as you said, a stubborn man. Molly has visited whenever possible, so little Angus knows her well. If the time comes and he can go to his proper home, Molly will have no problems in looking after him. In fact, she would love it, wouldn't you Molly?"

The house girl hugged the baby to her bosom.

"I loved Madam Lisa very much. I would be honoured and proud to look after her son. Boss Angus is a good man. At the moment he is feeling very angry at what life has done to him, but I know when he sees his son the ice that surrounds his heart will melt. He will become the other Angus that we know, a loving kind man who will be a wonderful father," and Molly kissed the copper curls tickling her nose. "Yes, little one. You need your father and your father needs you."

Penny glanced at her watch. She had fifteen minutes to get back to the hotel.

"Madam Rivas, thank you so much for everything. I'll do what I can to convince Angus to visit his child. Molly, it was fate working, allowing us to meet today. We'll work to get Boss Angus and his son together. Now, I must hurry, as I'm to meet Chris back at the hotel at one. I don't think I'll mention anything to him yet. Goodbye, baby Angus," and dropped a kiss onto his curls.

"Molly, Madam Rivas, I'll be in touch."

Penny hurried back to the hotel, her mind racing with ideas. Angus has to see his son. She couldn't help thinking what a waste of a year, but how rewarding it would be to reunite the two.

She ran up the steps to the hotel's entrance and waved at Chris, already seated near the swan fountain.

"Two minutes late, Penny," he admonished with a smile, pulling out a chair for her.

"I'm sorry Chris. Time ran away from me. Jinja is a fascinating place. I could wander around all day."

"Well, we don't have all day as I'm starving and the picnic basket is calling. I've had enough bricks, mortar, window frames, cement, sand and anything else that's needed for the extension to last me a lifetime. Let's go to the Owen Falls Dam and enjoy the scenery whilst we have lunch. As you can see," and the doctor pointed to a bottle of Rivas's special brew on the table, "I've organised refreshment."

They were soon bowling along the road towards the dam, Chris making light of the hassles thrown at him by the suppliers.

"When I'm convinced I've sorted everything out, bang, excuses pour out of their mouths as to why the building materials haven't arrived, excuses ranging from floods to droughts. It's enough to drive anybody crazy, but that's enough of my moaning. What did you do and see in your couple of hours?"

Penny sat quiet for a moment. Should she or shouldn't she tell the doctor about visiting Angus's child?

Not yet, she decided. *What a lovely surprise it will be for Chris when he finds out Angus has accepted the child as his own. Chris hasn't told me about the baby or Angus's accusations, so I don't want to embarrass him.*

"I loved the street sellers. What an amazing array of goods they have to sell," and Penny went into detail, describing all she'd seen.

Chris enjoyed listening to his love. She had the ability to bring things to life in her narrative and her enthusiasm soon dispelled his frustration.

Penny is definitely the one I want to spend the rest of my life with, he thought, whilst helping the nurse unpack the picnic basket on a small kopje overlooking the falls.

She has a quiet strength, which her patients recognise and love, but also a fragile vulnerability plucking at my heartstrings making me want to love and protect her from anything or anyone hurting her. She is truthfulness to her very core and I still can't believe my huge good fortune meeting her. I will always remember that day I knocked you off your feet and straight into my heart, Penny Whickam," and the doctor smiled at the nurse as she handed him a plate of snacks.

"Did you know the Owen Falls Dam is fed by the White Nile?" he asked, leaning back against a large rock, sipping fruit juice as they enjoyed the view of shimmering water reflecting the deep azure shade of the sky.

Penny shook her head. "I didn't know there was a White Nile. I've heard of the Nile of course, but a white one is news to me."

"Let me give you a short geography lesson. You'll be amazed to know there are several Niles. The White Nile rises from Lake Victoria, found on the borders of Tanzania, Kenya and Uganda, and its claim to fame is it's the second largest freshwater lake in the world. It then flows north and westward through Uganda, Lake Kyoga and Lake Albert where it's known as the Albert Nile. It then flows north to Nimule where it enters Sudan and becomes known as the Mountain Nile. And lastly, if I remember rightly, it flows over rapids entering the Sudan plain before meeting with the Blue Nile at Khartoum in Sudan forming the Nile you are familiar with. It's a huge river, about 2,300 miles long. And here endeth the geography lesson for today because I have more important things to do."

He raised his glass for a toast.

"Here's to providence that enabled me to meet the dove," and he clinked Penny's glass before leaning over and planting the tenderest of kisses on her soft lips.

That simple act fuelled his ardour. He placed his glass beside the rock, and gathering Penny into his arms, kissed her ardently but tenderly, tasting the sweetness of the juice on her lips, feeling her body respond to his love making until, breathless, they pulled apart, Penny's eyes huge and shining as she searched the doctor's face.

"Oh, Chris. I do love you so much. Sister Mercy was right, although I refused to believe her."

"Sister Mercy! Now what has Sister Mercy to do with anything?"

"She'd guessed how you felt about me that time ago. I said it was her imagination, but she wasn't having any of it. She said she's never wrong in her intuitions. I'll have to apologise to her."

"That will be soon, I hope. I want everyone to know how I feel about you."

Penny shivered. She still hadn't told Clair.

Tonight I will tell Clair about my love for Chris and his love for me. I will not put it off any longer, otherwise, it will just get harder and harder to do.

"Where are you, my love?" asked Chris, puzzled at the sudden stillness of Penny's body, and the set expression on her face. Surely she wasn't thinking of Angus?

Her face softened into a smile as she looked at the man she adored.

"Sorry, Chris. That expression of someone walking over my grave came to mind then. I would love to stay here for ever, but I suppose we should think about making tracks for home?"

Chris slid his arm around her slim waist and pulled her against him.

"Well, there's just something I need to do first, if that's all right with you, Nurse Whickam. It does concern you, or, to be more precise, your very inviting lips. They are begging to be kissed again, and as I would hate to disappoint them, you'll have to be patient for a while," and before Penny could answer, Doctor Chris Maynard was kissing her slowly and thoroughly.

Chapter Sixteen

Clair shrewdly smiled.

She watched Penny climb into the land rover with Chris, knowing they were heading for Jinja.

Our little nurse is on her mercy trip, and knowing the dove, she's going to hunt down the baby and try to come up with a plan to reunite Angus and his kid. That's fine. All I have to do is arrange things so Chris will believe Penny is doing all this because she loves Angus. My poor doctor. He'll be heartbroken to start with, of course, but I'll be there to comfort him. It won't take long before he's eating out of my hand like a little puppy. Chris will soon realise I'm the one he really loves. The lying dove will soon be forgotten.

Clair went to the ward, her mind planning her next move.

And it's time I paid Mother Superior another little visit. It won't hurt to add on a few more juicy titbits to the last conversation I had with her. Hopefully I'll have the chance this evening after tea. A few stories about Chris's misconduct as told to me by Penny can only enhance my cause.

Clair smirked as she assisted a patient into a wheel chair.

I'm looking forward to seeing Penny fall flat on her face, squirming. She won't know what's hit her.

The nurse's shift finally ended.

Clair walked across the courtyard to the dining room to have tea. She saw the land rover arrive, and waved as Penny clambered out.

"Hi Chris, hi Penny. Did you have a good day? How's Jinja?"

"Brilliant!" replied Penny. "The town's fascinating. You'll love it, Clair. Next time we'll go together."

Chris removed the picnic basket and carried it towards the dining room, saying he would see the girls later.

Penny turned to her friend, an apprehensive look on her face, her stomach churning in anticipation of the unpleasant ordeal ahead. She knew she couldn't put off telling the nurse about her feelings for the doctor any longer, and she wasn't looking forward to it one bit. She took a deep breath and said, "Clair, have you a minute to spare? There's something I must tell you."

"Yes, of course I do. What is it? You look very serious."

"Let's take a walk," and Penny led the way to the alcove and stood facing her friend.

"Clair, I've something to tell you, and as there's no easy way to do it, I'm just going to say it. I love Chris, and he loves me."

Silence.

"I'm so very sorry, Clair. I know just what Chris means to you, and I've fought against these feelings for so long, but I just couldn't help falling in love with him. I had no idea he felt the same."

Penny looked anxiously at the silent nurse standing in front of her.

"Clair, please say something, anything. I realise you probably hate me now, but I hope, over time, you'll see it in your heart to forgive me. I'm so very, very sorry, but there's nothing I can do to stop the way I feel."

Even though Clair had guessed what Penny wanted to say, to actually hear the words spoken sent a multitude of tiny daggers shooting through her body, causing small frissons of pain to accumulate, until her whole being screamed in agony. It took all of Clair's self control not to grab the nurse's throat and strangle the life out of her.

She closed her eyes, swallowed hard and pictured Penny's ultimate humiliation in front of the doctor. The sight soothed Clair's agony and she opened her eyes and looked at her rival.

"Don't look so guilty, Penny. I realise it's just a one- way street for Chris and me. He's never looked at me the way he does you. I hope you'll be very happy. No, don't cry," as Penny's eyes filled with tears. "I appreciate you telling me before I heard it from anybody else."

Clair gave Penny a hug and suggested going to the dining room to have tea.

"It's O.K. You've told me and now I must move on. Come, we can still be friends, can't we?"

"Oh, Clair, thank you for taking the news like this. I worried so much you would hate me. You really are a true friend. Now I can stop feeling guilty. Thank you," and hugged her colleague, before turning and walking out of the alcove.

Penny would've been stunned at the malicious look taking control of Clair's features, a look of undiluted loathing, aimed at her back and disappearing as quickly as it came, when Penny glanced over her shoulder and waved.

Once tea was over, Clair told Penny she had letters to write before retiring.

"That's fine Clair. I'll see you in the morning. I've news about Angus's son, which will please you, but I'll fill you in later. I know I'm going to need your help so I'll chat to you about the situation when we have our break under the tree."

Clair watched Penny walk away towards the staff's quarters, and then went to hunt down Mother Superior.

She was in her office, and invited the nurse inside.

"You look upset, Clair. Is anything the matter?"

"Yes, there is, Mother Superior. I hate having to come to you like this, but I've no other option."

"Well, if you've something on your mind, you know you can tell me in confidence. What ever is said in this office stays here, you know that."

"Yes, Mother Superior, I know, because I remember the last time I was here and, unfortunately, the reason I needed to speak to you then, is why I'm here now."

Clair stopped talking and looked down at her folded hands.

Sister Magdalene felt her heart sink. She hadn't forgotten the content of the conversation she'd had with Clair a while ago, but as nothing substantial had materialized, she'd hoped it was all a storm in a teacup and had dismissed it from her mind.

She looked at Clair with misgiving and asked her to continue.

"Well, Sister Magdalene, I don't know if you know Penny went with Doctor Maynard to Jinja today."

"Yes, Clair, I was aware of the trip."

The nurse shuffled in her seat, as though reluctant to continue.

"Come on, Clair. Please! What is it you want to say?" Mother Superior sounded exasperated.

It all came out in a rush.

"When Penny came back, she asked me to take a walk with her to the alcove, you know, the one with the bench in it, surrounded by bougainvillea. She said she had to speak to me privately as she was scared and didn't want Doctor Maynard to hear her. I asked her what was wrong and she started sobbing, really sobbing saying Doctor Maynard had forced her to go to Jinja and then made advances of a sexual nature to her and had become really angry when she rebuffed him. He threatened to have her sacked if she didn't accept his advances. Personally, I don't believe a word of it, but I told her she had to speak to you immediately, because this couldn't go on, but she wouldn't, Sister Magdalene. She said it had to stay between the two of us, and she felt better now that she'd spoken about it, and would put it out of her mind. She said she would make sure she wasn't alone with Doctor Maynard again, and then the strangest thing happened. Penny stopped sobbing and within seconds was smiling and joking as though the conversation had never happened. It was most bizarre."

Clair looked intently at Mother Superior.

"I'm worried about Doctor Maynard's reputation, Sister Magdalene. So far, Penny has only told me these fanciful stories, but what happens if she decides to take other people in her confidence. I know none of what she is saying is true, but others might believe her lies. She is amazingly convincing."

Mother Superior was aghast. For this to be happening again! It didn't make any sense.

"Right, Clair. Leave it with me. I'm sure you realise I don't need to tell you not to utter a word of this to anybody."

"Of course, Sister Magdalene. I wouldn't dream of saying anything. You can trust me, I promise."

"Right. Thank you for telling me. I realise it took courage for you to come here, and you did the right thing. Off you go now. I need to think and pray about the whole situation."

Clair immediately left the office, and then punched the air with her fist in triumph.

"Another point scored against the dove," she whispered, before heading to the staff quarters.

CHAPTER SEVENTEEN

It was mid morning of the next day, and the two nurses were sitting under the baobab tree drinking mango juice.

A heavy down pour an hour earlier had spring- cleaned away the dust, giving a magical glitter to the surrounding flora, the cerise blossoms of the bougainvillea in particular looking spectacular.

"Isn't this too lovely for words," said Penny, stretching out her legs, and leaning back in her chair sipping on her straw. "I just love this country."

"Yes, it's very nice, but you said last night you had news about the baby, so come on, out with it. You've kept me in suspense long enough."

Penny straightened up and placed her now empty glass on the table.

"I had such a piece of good fortune, Clair. After arriving in Jinja, Chris went off on some business to do with the extension giving me the chance to go to the town hall to see if I could trace the baby but the clerk wasn't interested in helping, as I hadn't any authorisation. She was right of course, and I knew it was a long shot, but even so, I felt disappointed. However", and Penny paused dramatically, "as I stood at the top of the steps of the town hall wondering what to do next, guess who I saw?"

"I haven't a clue. Who did you see?"

"Molly!"

"Molly? You mean Angus's Molly, the house girl?"

"Yes! As soon as I saw her, I realised she'd be the one to ask."

Penny grinned at her friend and continued, "She took me to meet the foster mother and the baby, and Clair, the baby is the spitting image of Angus. They're like two peas in a pod, same colour hair, everything, even down to the baby having Angus's temper apparently. I didn't see any evidence of that though. He seems such a happy natured child. But I tell you Clair, once Angus sees him, he'll know without any doubt he's the father, not Chris."

"This is great news, Penny. Well done. And what luck to meet Molly like that. It was meant to be, that's for sure. So, what to do next?"

"I spoke to Madam Rivas, she's the foster mum, and a good friend of Chris; she said it would be lovely if Angus met the child. She'd always hoped he would change his mind and acknowledge the baby as his. I suggested maybe we could persuade Angus to go to Jinja, but Madam Rivas felt it would be better if Molly took the baby to the plantation so that Angus could become acquainted on home ground so to speak. We just need to work out the details."

"Does Chris know about your little expedition?"

"No, not yet. I thought it best not to say anything until Angus sees his child, and hopefully, realise he's the father and not Chris. Then we'll have really good news to tell him. What do you think?"

"I agree. Best not to say anything until it's a forgone conclusion."

Clair finished her fruit juice and stood up.

"Guess it's time to go back to the salt mine. You did well, Penny. We must discuss the next plan of action soon. I'll see you at lunch."

Penny looked fondly at Clair as she waved to her before disappearing through the doors of the men's ward.

"To think I was apprehensive at seeing Clair this morning after the bombshell I gave her last night. I needn't have worried. She's been great," and Penny walked to her ward with a light heart, delighted at the way everything was turning out.

If only she'd known what the future had in store, Penny would've taken the first flight back to England immediately.

It was seven-thirty in the evening, and the cooks were busy preparing a barbecue for the staff and those patients able to eat outside.

The evening was balmy, the temperature having dropped to a pleasant 25degrees, and for once, the air felt dry instead of moist. The sun had set, leaving streaks of crimson, gold, pink and orange shooting across the sky, the inspiration of an artist who'd picked the colours and thrown them at a canvas. The resulting work of art was magnificent.

"This sunset is stunning. I've never seen anything like this in England," Penny said to Clair, as they walked back to their chairs carrying plates of barbecued meat and salad. "It must be something to do with cleaner air as there's no industrial smoke, and of course, less light that let's us see things more clearly. I've certainly noticed many more stars than I ever saw in England."

Clair finished chewing on her barbecued rib, glazed with a mango chutney and mayonnaise sauce. She nodded in agreement, and reached for a serviette to wipe her lips and fingers.

"Yes, it's all very lovely, but we must concentrate on getting Angus and the baby together... shh, here comes Chris. We don't want him to know what's going on yet. Hi Chris, I see you've also gone for the delicious ribs. The sauce is out of this world."

Doctor Maynard smiled at the two nurses and then sat down next to Penny, whose heart raced, whilst a delicious blush enhanced her stunning eyes as she glanced at the doctor before concentrating on her food.

"My favourite," he answered, holding one aloft. He intercepted Penny's glance with one of his own, love flowing from his eyes to hers, causing her heart to beat even faster, making her breathless.

Quiet ensued as the trio ate, but Clair had noticed the glance between Chris and Penny. Jealousy formed a tight knot in her stomach destroying her appetite for food but fanning her appetite for revenge.

She thought hard, planning the next moves on her chess- board of hate.

The game drew closer to check mate the next day with additional help Mother Superior unwittingly supplied.

But in the interim, Clair was on the look out for Thomas the driver, who just happened to be Molly's son. The nurse had learnt this interesting snippet of information by chatting to Rebecca, Thomas's girlfriend.

The next morning, walking to her ward, Clair saw the young man cleaning one of the land rovers.

"Good morning Thomas. Working hard I see!"

The driver gave the nurse a beaming smile, black skin contrasting sharply against his white teeth.

"That's right, Nurse Clair. Too much mud from rains. Job too hard," and Thomas rolled his eyes heavens ward, giving Clair a startling view of just the whites.

"Thomas, can I ask you something?"

"Of course, Nurse Clair."

"When are you next visiting your mother? Is it soon?"

Thomas laughed. "Very soon. I am seeing my mother this afternoon."

"That's good, as I have a letter for Boss Angus. Would you please give it to him?"

"Of course, Nurse Clair."

Clair handed Thomas the letter. "And when will you return to The Haven?"

"This evening. Doctor Chris said I could use the land rover because he needs me tomorrow."

"That's great. I expect Boss Angus will have a reply for me, so if he has, I shall be in my room. You will find me there."

She smiled at the driver and continued walking to her ward.

"That's a stroke of luck. Hopefully Angus will do what I've asked in the letter. Then all I have to do is manoeuvre Chris and Penny to where I want them to be, and bingo! Let's see the sparks fly.

That evening Thomas handed Clair a letter from the plantation owner.

She read it quickly, a smile of satisfaction crossing her face.

"Excellent, that's just perfect. Now to find Chris."

Poor Sister Magdalene. She'd thought long and hard about the conversation she'd had with Clair, and knew the time had arrived to speak to Doctor Maynard about Penny's accusations. She had thought of confronting the nurse first, but decided against it, as she didn't want to jeopardise Clair's friendship. This was a decision she would heartily regret.

It was just after supper and Sister Magdalene saw her favourite doctor walking towards his office.

I have to speak to him sooner or later, so let it be now and get it over and done with, she decided, and called his name.

The doctor turned, saw the nun waving to him, and hurried over to her, concerned at the anxious expression on her face.

"Is there anything wrong, Sister? You look upset."

"Yes, something is wrong, Chris. Do you have five minutes to spare? I need to discuss a state of affairs that has developed."

"If it's about the extension, you needn't worry. Everything seems to be back on track at long last. I realise it's taken longer than we envisaged, but there's no accounting for African time."

"No, Chris. It has nothing to do with the extension. How I wish it were. Come, let's go to my office."

Mystified, the doctor followed Mother Superior to her office and accepted a seat facing opposite her.

"I'm not sure how to start this conversation, Chris, so I'll come straight to the point. According to information I've received, Penny has said you've sexually harassed her."

"What!"

Doctor Maynard jumped up from his chair.

"Penny has said what?"

"Now calm down Chris. I obviously don't believe a word, but it has come to my ears that this is what Penny's been saying."

"Who told you such rubbish?"

"I'm sorry. I can't divulge that. What I am worried about is although I realise there can be no grounds for such accusations, if this gets round The Haven and outside, it can badly damage your reputation. So, I'm asking you to tread circumspectly until I get to the bottom of these stories. I will be speaking to Penny of course, but I wanted to warn you first."

Doctor Maynard was shaken to the core. He had dismissed the first inklings of these accusations out of hand, believing Clair had heard wrongly, but now! His beautiful, sweet, caring Penny saying such things? No, not in a million years. Something was very wrong.

"Now Chris, I don't want you saying anything to Penny. Let me have a word with her first. All I'm asking is for you to be very careful until I get to the truth of these accusations."

Chris was pacing the floor, but stopped dead at these words.

"But how can you ask that of me, Sister Magdalene? Of course I must speak to Penny! There's no way she would ever say anything like that about me. I'm sure you've guessed how I feel about her. You must know I love her and I know the feeling is mutual!"

Mother Superior grasped the doctor by his arms. "Please, Chris. Just for now don't say anything. Stay away from Penny until we know exactly what's going on. It would be far better for me to get to the bottom of these allegations. We need to be totally discreet. Mud sticks, you know it does!"

Chris stared at the nun. What she was asking went totally against everything he stood for, honesty and transparency. But was she right? Would he do more harm than good by confronting Penny?

He came to a decision. "I will do what you ask, Sister Magdalene. I will stay away from Penny for now. I don't agree with you but I won't say anything, yet." And the doctor strode out of the office.

The last person he wanted to see was Clair, but there she was, waiting near the entrance, hovering like a bee.

"I'm so glad to have bumped into you, Chris. I need to ask you a favour."

"Not now Clair. Maybe later?"

"No problem, Chris. Can I see you in your office say just after six tomorrow evening? I won't take up too much of your time."

"Fine, I'll see you then," and the doctor strode off.

Clair's green eyes glistened like a cat as she put two and two together.

"Chris has had a chat with Sister Magdalene, and boy, is he upset, but it seems the good Mother Superior has kept my name out of it, otherwise he would've said something. Clair, my girl, this is going so perfectly. Now, let me visit the dove and manoeuvre her into position."

Penny was in her room writing a letter to her parents.

If I can convince my mother lions are not roaming the streets of Jinja and that sanitation does not consist of a bucket, she and dad may be persuaded to come out to Uganda for a holiday. It will be lovely to see them and introduce them to Chris.

Penny stopped writing, her thoughts drifting to her love and the magical moments spent together. She couldn't help smiling as she remembered the words of love Chris had spoken to her, the thrill of his kisses sending pulses of desire pulsating through her body, leaving her breathless.

She gave herself a mental shake. *Stop right now, Penny, otherwise this letter will never get written*, and picked up her pen just as Clair knocked on her door.

"Hi, Penny, it's only me. I'm not disturbing you, am I?"

"Of course not Clair. Come in. I'm just writing a letter to my parents."

Clair walked over to Penny's bed and sat down.

"I've good news. Angus is coming to The Haven at six tomorrow evening. I've arranged for us to meet him in the alcove, as it's nice and secluded there. We don't want any prying eyes seeing us."

"But that's right opposite Chris's office, Clair. You know he often works until supper time."

"Not a problem, Penny. I heard Chris say to Sister Magdalene earlier he wanted to check on the follow up care given to some ex-patients living in one of the villages near the river. He's leaving in the afternoon so won't be back for supper. We'll have plenty of time to talk with Angus and persuade him to see his child. Chris will be delighted when we tell him the good news."

Penny smiled, imagining the joyful reunion of the Scotsman and his son, and the barriers breaking down between Angus and her darling doctor.

"Oh, I so hope everything works out well, Clair. How wonderful it will be for Angus to find happiness again, and for his and Chris's friendship to get back on track."

"Absolutely, Penny. Six o'clock tomorrow evening will be the defining moment in the grand scheme of things. I can't wait!" and Clair hugged Penny before wishing her good night.

CHAPTER EIGHTEEN

Penny was distraught.

Chris had totally ignored her and she had no idea why.

How her heart leapt with joy seeing the doctor walk into the ward. However, he made his way to the office where Sister Mercy sat at her desk updating care plans. But Penny wasn't worried. She knew Chris would soon stride over to where she was helping Ruth with her baby, and her heart hammered in her chest at the expectation of looking into his dark blue eyes and feel love radiate from them as he looked down at her.

Her dismay when he walked away from the office and hurried out of the ward without a backward glance was too much to bear.

Disappointment enveloped her.

She gently lifted the now sweet smelling baby and handed her to her mother, who held out her arms, the new prosthetic hands attached.

Don't be silly, Penny, she admonished herself. *Chris is a busy man, and besides, he's worrying about the extension that's taking too long to build, and money is getting short, but that doesn't explain why he only said a curt hullo this morning at breakfast. What on earth did I do to warrant that?*

Once Ruth was settled, Penny slowly made her way to the office where she asked Sister Mercy if she could have an earlier break as she had a splitting headache.

"Of course, my dear," said the nun. "You are looking peaky. As the work is all up to date, why don't you have a lie down in your room

for a while? It's exceptionally hot today. Maybe the heat is getting to you," and she gave Penny a sympathetic smile before shooing her off the ward saying she would call her if she was needed.

As Penny disappeared through the ward entrance, Sister Mercy shook her head.

True love is not running smoothly between our doctor and the dove. I've never seen Chris look the way he did when he came to the office just now. Not even during the problems with Angus McFadden and poor Lisa dying. Something drastic has happened between him and Penny. I wonder what's going on?

The doctor in question hurried to his office and flung himself down in his chair, thoughts and emotions in turmoil as he ran his fingers through his hair, wanting desperately to speak to Penny about the accusations she had supposedly spoken but unable to do so because of his promise to Sister Magdalene.

"I don't believe any of it," he muttered furiously. "This is all a huge misunderstanding, and regardless whether Sister Magdalene has said anything to Penny by tonight or not, I will speak to her and clear up this mess." He groaned to himself. "I love you so much, Penny. You are my life. I just can't imagine living without you. None of this makes any sense." He banged his fist on the desk in frustration, pens rattling in protest. "Yes, tonight I'll speak to my love and get this mess sorted out."

Penny, meanwhile, lay on her bed under the mosquito netting, tears falling onto her pillow as she hugged it to herself for comfort. "Why am I putting myself through this again?" she mumbled to the pillow in anguish. "Didn't I suffer enough in England? Tonight I'll go to Chris and demand an explanation as to why he's ignoring me. Oh, I forgot. He's going to that village later. Well, tomorrow will have to do. Hopefully I'll have good news for him regarding Angus and everything will be sorted out. I love you so much, Chris. I can't imagine my life without you." and Penny slipped into an emotionally exhausted dreamless sleep.

She awoke to knocking on her door.

"Penny, Penny are you there? Can I come in?"

It was Clair saying it was nearly six, time for Penny to be in the alcove, as Angus would be arriving any minute.

"Goodness, I didn't realise I'd slept that long. Sorry Clair. Give me a minute."

"No problem. I'll meet you there. There's something I have to do first. I won't be long."

Clair checked her watch; five minutes to six.

Angus had already concealed himself in the alcove, hiding behind a bougainvillea bush so Chris didn't see him before time. Having read Clair's letter, appraising him of the plan, he was quite happy to bide his time before putting the doctor's downfall into action. After all, what are a few more minutes after he'd been waiting a year for this opportunity?

Darkness fell at six, as Clair knew it would. She became impatient waiting for Penny.

Ah! At last. Here she comes. I recognise those footsteps. Careful, I mustn't let Penny see me. Chris, I know, is in his office, although why he's sitting in the dark is a mystery. But that's worked out perfectly. Penny will continue to believe Chris is still away at the village. The light from the moon will be perfect, better in fact.

Clair watched as Penny hurried to the alcove and then disappeared from view.

Right. Now to visit Doctor Maynard.

Penny, meanwhile, stopped by the seat, and looked around her.

The moon cast shadows from the surrounding bushes so she didn't see Angus slip out of his hideaway until he stood a few feet away.

"Hullo Penny."

Penny quickly turned to see Angus standing behind her, his face in shadows, but his eyes glittering in the moon- light.

"Oh, you startled me, Angus. But I'm so glad you were able to come. Shall we sit on the seat? I know Clair will be here any minute now," and Penny sat down, patting the space beside her.

They sat in silence for a few moments, Penny at a lost as to what to say as she realised she hadn't asked Clair how much her friend had told Angus about why he was here.

Angus, content to say nothing as he watched out for Clair's signal, surreptitiously slid an arm behind Penny's shoulders, letting it rest on the back of the seat.

Finally Penny broke the silence.

"Angus, I don't know where Clair is, but the reason we have to speak to you is because I went to Jinja and saw the baby…"

That was all she was able to say before Angus suddenly swept her into his arms, pulling her body hard against his and kissed her firmly on the mouth.

Penny, stunned into immobility at this turn of events, didn't start struggling for a few moments and then when she did, Angus immediately let go, stood up, and in a loud voice said, "I knew you felt the same way, Penny. We'll talk again very soon my love," and strode out of the alcove and disappeared into the dark.

Penny stayed sitting, staring blindly in front of her.

Then Chris arrived on the scene, shaking with anger, revulsion and contempt in equal measures spewing out of his mouth.

"So, the dove has turned into a back- stabbing, lying vulture has she. No! Don't even try and say anything. Nothing you say will ever right all the wrongs you have done to me. And to think I loved you! Now I only feel loathing and disgust! How could you do this to me?" and the doctor turned on his heels and stormed away.

Penny was galvanised into action.

"Chris," she cried, "wait, please wait. I can explain. Please Chris," and ran after him, grasping his arm to slow down his desperate pace.

"Don't touch me," he growled. "Just get out of my sight," and he strode through his office door, slamming it shut behind him.

Penny stood staring at the closed door, her world rapidly gone crazy, not knowing what to do or what to say, not understanding anything that had happened.

She felt a tap on her shoulder and turned to see Clair standing a few feet behind her.

"Sorry I'm late, Penny. I got held up, but what are you doing here? We have to meet Angus in the alcove." (This said quietly so that Chris didn't hear.)

Penny opened her mouth to speak but nothing came out. She tried again, but still no sounds were possible. Disbelief had immobilised her; Penny was incapable of doing or saying anything.

Clair was all concern.

"What's going on Penny? You look awful. Something dreadful has happened, hasn't it? I'll just tell Angus to wait a while," and turned as though to go to the alcove.

"He's gone," whispered Penny.

"What do you mean, he's gone? Have you already spoken to him? What did he say? asked Clair, her voice a perfect blend of surprise and bewilderment.

Penny just shook her head.

Clair looked at the nurse, inwardly delighting at how perfect her plan had worked. It was hard keeping a straight face when confronted with the horrified expression on Penny's, but she managed it, and soothingly took the shocked nurse by the arm and led her to the staff quarters, where she helped Penny into bed, brought her a hot drink of Horlicks, having surreptitiously slipped a sleeping tablet into the liquid and sat with her until she fell into a traumatized sleep.

Clair waited a few minutes to make sure Penny was sleeping, and then slipped out of the room, grinning broadly, and walked quickly but quietly back to the alcove.

"Angus," she whispered. "Angus, are you still here?"

Angus moved silently out of the shadows.

"Careful," whispered Clair. "We don't want Chris to see us."

"No need to worry about that," said her partner in crime. "I saw him leave his office and drive off in his land rover. I must say he looked mightily upset."

"And so he would be, seeing his dove showing her true colours. She's a lying scheming bitch who only has herself to blame."

Clair hugged herself, savouring the moment when she raised her arm as though to swat a mosquito as she stood behind Chris. He was staring out of the office window looking at Penny and Angus, illuminated by the moon – light, sitting very cosily together on the seat. She could still hear his sudden intake of breath as he watched Angus sweep Penny into his arms and soundly kiss her.

"No, no, this can't be happening. Why is she doing this to me? Why? Why?"

His voice getting louder and louder, the doctor raced out of the office and ran around the corner to the alcove, too late to see Angus disappearing in the darkness, but able to stand in front of a stunned Penny, shaking with anger as he vented his horror and disbelief.

Oh, how Clair had enjoyed witnessing that scene.

How perfect everything went. Clair, my girl, you are a genius. Now all you have to do is be around to pick up the pieces, be a consoling shoulder for Chris to cry on. He will soon realise I'm the one he truly loves; Penny was just a shallow fling. Yes, Chris, we shall live very happily together for the rest of our lives.

"If you can stop gloating for just a minute," said Angus, "there's something I want to ask you."

"What's that?"

"Just before I kissed her, Penny said something about seeing a baby. What did she mean? What baby?"

Damn, thought Clair. *I thought I told Penny to wait for me before she said anything about the kid. Angus mustn't know about her little expedition.*

"I haven't a clue. Maybe she thought you would be interested in Ruth's baby. Ruth's one of your workers, isn't she?"

"Yes, she is. I expect that's it. Still, I thought she mentioned Jinja, but I can't be certain, as I was keeping my eyes open for your signal, without Chris realising what I was up to. Anyway, it's time for me to leave. I parked my land rover outside the compound so Chris wouldn't see it. I'll be in touch," and the plantation owner walked away, somehow not feeling as elated as he thought he would at seeing Chris emotionally torn apart.

The same couldn't be said for Clair.

She went to her room in a state of euphoria. Chris's reaction was exactly what she'd hoped for, and more. Now all she had to do was show the doctor she was there for him and let him know her love was strong and true, not shallow and self- seeking like Penny's. He would soon forget the other nurse, realising the difference between the infatuation he had for her and the overwhelming love he would soon feel for Clair.

Her sense of triumph grew substantially the next day after hearing Penny had received a summons to Mother Superior's office.

CHAPTER NINETEEN

Following a restless sleep, Penny awoke, believing she'd dreamt the evening's events. Then the harsh truth of reality swept in like a tidal wave, and she realised that no, she hadn't been dreaming, Chris really had said those incredibly hurtful words.

She pulled the bed- clothes closer to her chin, hugging them tightly as waves of misery swept over her. Tears welled up and spilled down her cheeks, soaking her pillow once more.

"This can't be happening again. How could everything go so wrong? I haven't done anything to be ashamed of and yet my world has shattered. Why did Angus kiss me like that? I know I didn't say or do anything to make him think I had those sort of feelings for him. What did I do to Chris even before last night to make him so angry with me, ignoring me the way he did? Nothing makes any sense?"

She hugged the pillow closer.

"Well, I guess this is as bad as it gets," and Penny dragged herself out of bed to have a shower and get ready for work.

The summons came during breakfast.

Penny had looked around to see if Chris was in the dining room, but the doctor was nowhere to be seen.

With sinking heart, she forced herself to eat a piece of toast. The bread turned to ashes in her mouth, and she pushed her plate away in disgust.

Clair hadn't made an appearance as she was due two days off, so the nurse remained sitting on her own, contemplating a sad and lonely future, when Sister Beatrice, a young nun who worked on the children's ward told Penny, Mother Superior would like to see her in the office when she'd finished her breakfast.

Penny smiled sadly at the nun and said she'd go immediately.

The nurse walked along the corridor towards Sister Magdalene's office, her mind searching the reason behind the summons.

Mother Superior has heard how angry Chris is with me. Maybe she knows what's happened and is going to explain.

Penny stopped walking; hope soared into her heart, putting a smile back on her face.

Yes, that's it. Sister Magdalene will tell me there's been a huge misunderstanding and Chris is in her office right now, ready to apologise and hug me and tell me everything is fine, and how stupid he's been, and with lifting spirits she hurried to the door.

Five minutes later, Penny sat staring at the nun, unable to think clearly as she tried to absorb the words Mother Superior had just spoken.

"I'm sorry Sister Magdalene. Could you please repeat that," she whispered, not believing she'd heard correctly, waves of nausea sweeping over her, as the enormity of the words continued to reverberate in her ears.

"I said, Nurse Whickam, I've had several reports saying you told a member of staff Doctor Maynard has been making a nuisance of himself in a sexual manner, and that he said if you didn't give in to his advances you would be fired."

"But Sister Magdalene, none of it is true! I love Chris with all of my heart. Why would I say such things about him! He is the kindest, gentlest, most wonderful man I've ever met. Who told you I said these things? I need to know! Who would say such awful lies about me, and why?"

Mother Superior was in a quandary.

Penny appeared genuinely shocked and horrified at what had been said, but the nun had given her word not to reveal her source, and as Clair had told her early this morning about Penny's conduct with Angus McFadden last night, this could be the proof she needed to see Penny could be a very good actress who enjoyed creating drama and discord.

Poor Doctor Maynard. He'd phoned from Jinja to inform the nun he would be away for a few days. Not one word did he say about Penny's misconduct with Angus McFadden, but Mother Superior read between the lines. She heard the despair in Chris's voice and her heart hardened towards this young woman who played with her favourite doctor's emotions like this in such a callous way.

"I know this may sound harsh, Nurse Whickam, but I think it would be best if you went back to England for a while until things settle down."

"But Sister Magdalene, I haven't done anything wrong! I don't understand any of this. I haven't accused Chris of anything. I love him!"

"Then why were you kissing Angus McFadden in the alcove last night if you love Doctor Maynard so much?"

Penny stared at Mother Superior. How did she know about that?

"But I wasn't kissing him. He suddenly grabbed me and kissed me! I pushed him away."

"Obviously not quick enough as Doctor Maynard saw you together. I know you are a free spirit, Nurse Whickam, and I'm not condemning you for finding Angus attractive, but I really thought you had something very special between you and Doctor Maynard. You have been extremely foolish to have thrown that away, unless you weren't serious about the relationship in the first place. But, if you weren't, then you have treated the doctor very shabbily. Another thing I do not understand is why Angus McFadden was here last night. If you have no feelings for him why did you have an assignation with him?"

"Because of his baby, Sister Magdalene. I saw baby Angus in Jinja, and he looks so much like his father. I knew Angus thought Chris was the father, so I wanted Angus to see the child. I know when he does he'll see immediately the huge resemblance between himself and his son. I just wanted to bring them together and hopefully restore the friendship between the two men. Oh, what an awful mess this is.

But wait! Clair knows all about this. She actually arranged for Angus to be in the garden last night. Sister Magdalene, please, ask Clair what happened. She'll back me up. She'll tell you how she arranged for Angus to be here!"

"Nurse Dansbury knows nothing about it, Nurse Whickam. I've already asked her and she had no knowledge of the meeting between you and Angus."

Penny staggered, as though somebody had punched her in the stomach.

"But, that's not true," she stammered, "Clair arranged for Angus to be here. Why would she say otherwise! Please, ask Clair to come here. I know this is all a huge misunderstanding!"

"I can't do that. Nurse Dansbury has gone to Jinja with Thomas. She left early this morning saying she had some business to attend to. Fortunately, Thomas was able to give her a lift."

Penny's mind was in turmoil.

Clair had lied to Sister Magdalene about organising the arrangements for Angus to meet in the garden last night, and now she'd high tailed it to Jinja. What was going on?

"Can you contact Angus, Sister Magdalene? If you ask him who arranged the meeting, he'll tell you it was Clair, not me."

Mother Superior was ready with her trump card.

"I have already phoned him, Nurse Whickam. I obviously didn't go into any details, but he readily told me how you'd contacted him as you were missing him so much. Really, I have to say you have been playing fast and loose with the affections of both Doctor Maynard and Angus McFadden! I would never have believed it of you. I am bitterly disappointed in your conduct. I'm sorry; you are not the type of nurse I want at The Haven. The sooner arrangements are made for you to go back to England, the better. Now, please leave my office whilst I organise your departure. I have covered your shift on the ward, so I suggest you start packing your suitcases."

Penny was dismissed.

The unyielding expression on Mother Superior's face told the nurse protesting wouldn't get her anywhere. She slowly walked out of the office and blindly made her way back to her room where she flung herself down on her bed, a multitude of unanswered questions pounding her brain until she felt it would explode.

As she lay there, she forced herself to think rationally and clearly, and went step by step out loud through the preceding events and came to one conclusion.

"Clair! Clair has lied and lied about me. She's the one who told stories to Sister Magdalene about Chris and me. She convinced Angus to do what he did. She has orchestrated everything to destroy my relationship with Chris, and she has used Angus, who obviously went along with her for his own agenda, to get back at the person he's convinced destroyed his life. How blind and trusting I've been! I really thought Clair was my friend and had accepted the relationship between Chris and myself." Penny sadly shook her head. "How could I have been so brainless? And now Clair is on her way to Jinja so I can't even confront her."

She swung her legs to the floor and paced up and down the room.

"So, now what? How do I convince Chris and Sister Magdalene I'm telling the truth and it's Clair that's lying? Clair has Angus on her side. So, it's my word against both of theirs."

The situation appeared hopeless.

CHAPTER TWENTY

"You can drop me off here, Thomas. I'm staying at the hotel tonight and making my own way back to The Haven tomorrow."

Thomas drew up in front of the Flying Swan Hotel, and helped Clair with her over night bag. She waved goodbye and then turned to walk up the steps leading to the entrance.

Penny's description was spot on. This really is a lovely place, and there is the swan sculpture she raved over. Clair chuckled. *Poor baby! Her interview with Sister Magdalene is probably over and she could well be packing her bags, so good riddance to the conniving dove!*

Clair walked to reception, and booked a room for the night. As she turned to follow the porter, she couldn't believe her luck. There by the lift stood Doctor Maynard, talking to an Indian gentleman. *And to think I was worried about finding him in Jinja.*

"Chris!" she exclaimed. "What a surprise to see you. I didn't know you were in Jinja!"

The doctor turned sharply at hearing his name, his heart leaping in his chest when he thought it was Penny, but feeling it sink in hopelessness when he saw Clair.

Damn! Even after everything that has happened, I still love her with every fibre of my being. Will I ever be able to stop loving that girl, and struggled to compose his face into a smile.

"Hullo Clair. I didn't expect to see you here. Are you on your own?"

"Yes, I've two days off so I thought I would take advantage of the time to check out Jinja. Penny couldn't praise the town enough when she was telling me about her visit here with you, especially about this hotel."

Chris flinched when he heard Penny's name, an expression not gone unnoticed by Clair.

"I'm glad she enjoyed it," he said, his voice expressionless. "Let me introduce you to my friend Rivas. He's the owner of the hotel. Rivas, this is Clair, one of the nurses from England working at The Haven."

Rivas held out his hand.

"A pleasure to meet you, Miss Clair. I hope you are enjoying your stay in this country?"

"Very much so," replied the nurse. "I'm having a wonderful time, and it's so rewarding to work with the Ugandan people and feel that one is making a difference in their lives, however small that difference is. And of course, to work with someone like Chris is an added bonus," and smiled up at the doctor.

"Yes, well, thank you Clair."

"Duty calls, Chris. Don't forget your having dinner with us this evening. And, Miss Clair," said Rivas, turning towards the nurse, "you are more than welcome to join us. My wife enjoys meeting new people."

"I would love to. Thank you so much for inviting me," and Clair smiled happily at both men.

It just keeps getting better and better, she thought.

Rivas walked away leaving Clair and Chris standing by the lifts.

"Are you here on business?" Clair asked the doctor.

"No, I just needed to get away for a couple of days. Why do you ask?"

"Well, if you haven't anything planned, I really would appreciate you showing me around Jinja, as long as it wouldn't inconvenience you, of course. I don't want to be a nuisance."

Chris thought for a minute before replying.

This might be one way of taking his mind off Penny. After all, Clair has no idea what's been happening, and some uncomplicated company could be the answer. Being alone wasn't such a good idea.

"Of course I will, Clair. Get yourself settled in your room and I'll meet you at one of the tables by the flying swan fountain say in fifteen minutes. We'll have a drink and decide where to go."

"Excellent. I'll see you in fifteen," and Clair disappeared into the lift, her heart soaring at the same pace as the lift rushed to her floor.

Fifteen minutes later she was sitting opposite the doctor, sipping an ice- cold coke as Chris mentioned various places of interest. Clair had quickly freshened up and changed into a sky blue blouse and white slacks, which she knew complimented her looks. Putting on fresh makeup, and spraying her favourite perfume in strategic places, she realised this was a golden opportunity to impress Chris, and determined not to waste it.

"He'll soon forget Penny," she said aloud, picking her shoulder bag off the bed. "He'll realise she's just a flash in the pan. A little time spent with me, and Chris will recognise how shallow his feelings are for her. True love is what we have together," and sailed out of the door to keep the appointment with her one and only.

Chris, meanwhile, wished with all his heart he could put back the clock and have Penny sitting opposite him instead of Clair. He still couldn't grasp what had happened and found it difficult concentrating on Clair's chattering as the mental image of Penny clasped in Angus's arms kept swimming in front of his eyes.

"I'm sorry Clair. What did you say?"

"I said I would love to go to the Owen Falls Dam."

"No! I'm sorry, that was rude. If you don't mind, I would prefer to give the Falls a miss today. How about I show you around the town? It's a fascinating place with quite a history attached to it."

This was not exactly what Clair had in mind. Romance had been uppermost, preferably in a secluded, romantic setting where she could seduce the doctor and erase Penny totally from his mind. However, that opportunity would come later.

"That sounds great, Chris. Where shall we start?"

"Let's start walking, and I'll fill you in on the local history beginning with the fact that Jinja is twinned with Finchley in London since 1963. Did you know that Clair?"

"How fascinating. What else can you tell me?" a question Clair bitterly regretted as the doctor bombarded her with facts and figures about population size, and went into detail about the main languages being lusoga and ganda, plus his views on the fact the average income was only US$100 per annum, until Clair wanted to scream in frustration.

This isn't how I want to spend my time with Chris, she thought despairingly. *Who cares if the biggest employer is the Kakira Sugar Works. So it runs on sugar alcohol. Big deal! I couldn't give a damn.*

She grabbed hold of the doctor's hand and smiled up at him.

"Let's have a coffee over there," pointing to a coffee house, brightly coloured umbrellas standing sentry on the pavement, inviting passers by to sit under their protection from the sun and enjoy the wide variety of coffees Uganda had to offer.

If Clair thought the conversation would turn more intimate, she was doomed to disappointment. The doctor continued droning on and on about Jinja as though anaesthetising himself from thinking about anything else.

When it was time to go to the Rivas household, both parties were relieved.

I need to get Chris relaxed and a few glasses of wine should do the trick. Let's hope his friend and wife aren't teetotal. I want Chris in my bed tonight, come hell or high water. He will love me! I shall make him!

CHAPTER TWENTY ONE

As Molly swept the kitchen floor, the conversation she'd heard between her boss and Sister Magdalene played over and over in her head, like a stuck record.

She knew it was Mother Superior on the other end of the line because she'd answered the phone herself. Once she'd told Boss Angus about the call, she went back to the kitchen, but as the phone was in the hall that ran next to the kitchen, hearing what he had to say was easy. Normally, she wouldn't have taken any notice, but when she heard the dove's name mentioned and Boss Angus saying such things about his feelings towards her, Molly stopped what she was doing and listened harder.

None of it made any sense.

"Yes, Mother Superior. At least, that's what Penny told me. We were discussing our future together. Why? Has she said anything different?"

There was a pause in the conversation, and then Angus said, "Now why would she say that! Chris has never been mentioned in any of our chats. I don't understand! What is she trying to do? Play us off against each other?"

Another pause, then, "none of this makes any sense. I'm sure Penny loves me. I know she does. She told me so." Another pause, then, "I am devastated. I would never have guessed Penny could be so deceitful. Yes, I understand. Goodbye Mother Superior." and he replaced the receiver.

And then Molly heard the strangest thing of all.

"There you are, Clair. I hope that satisfies you." and Angus wandered off to the veranda.

Molly finished sweeping the floor, and then picked up her duster before walking into the lounge. As she passed the veranda, she glanced at her boss sitting in his favourite chair smoking, his gaze unseeing into the distance. He didn't look heart broken over his doomed affair with the dove! In fact, the opposite, triumph emanated from him.

Whilst flicking the duster around the lounge, Molly's confusion grew.

How could I be so wrong? she thought. *No, I don't believe I am wrong. Nurse Penny is sweet on Doctor Chris. Yes, she is friendly with Boss Angus and wants to see him united with his son, but only because she is a kind, caring person, not because she loves him. No, the dove loves Doctor Chris, but I don't understand. Why did Boss Angus say him and the dove are in love and then speak like that about Nurse Clair?*

Molly's dusting grew more frantic as her confusion grew.

I knew Nurse Clair is not a good lady. Is she trying to cause trouble for our dove?

The duster whipped around the room at a bewildering speed and the inevitable happened.

CRASH!

A wooden sculpture of a giraffe, standing unsteady at the best of times on the bookshelf, went flying and fell to the floor, causing Molly to jolt out of her reverie and Angus fly to his feet shouting at her to be more careful.

"Sorry, Boss Angus. Nothing broken," and the house girl gently replaced the giraffe, before giving up dusting as a bad job, and going back into the kitchen, where she immersed her arms in warm soapy water and scrubbed pots so clean she saw her reflection in them as she tried to decide what to do with the information she had, or whether she should do anything at all. After all, was it any of her business?

Molly abruptly stopped scrubbing. She had come to a decision.

I must speak to Mother Superior. Something very bad is happening to the dove and it's up to me, Molly Ndlovu, to stop it. Please let me be in time.

She went to Angus, still sitting in his chair smoking his pipe.

"Boss Angus, I need some shopping. I have left your lunch in the fridge. There are cold meats and a salad. When I get back I will cook your favourite meal."

"And what might that be, Molly?" asked Angus, a satisfied grin on his face.

"Mutton chops with a thick onion gravy."

"Excellent. Don't be too long," and the plantation owner resumed puffing on his pipe whilst idly fingering the ears of his dog.

Molly didn't hang around. Coat and hat on, she hurried to the main dirt road running parallel to the plantation, praying there would be some sort of transport she could use to get to The Haven as quickly as possible.

Luck was on her side. In the distance she saw dust clouds approaching.

She stepped into the middle of the road and flagged down a kombi owned by her friend David Sithole.

David stopped the vehicle and asked Molly where she wanted to go.

"The Haven," replied Molly as she clambered aboard.

"No problem. I'm going there anyway," said the driver.

She sat silently, contemplating her next move as they sped along the road, dirt clouds soaring high behind them, coating the foliage with a fine brown dust. Once they reached The Haven, David helped Molly step down from the kombi.

"Do you need a lift back home?" he asked. "I will be ready to leave in an hour."

Molly nodded. "Yes please David. I'll meet you here in an hour."

Her heart beating nineteen to the dozen, and a sick feeling in her stomach, Molly hurried to Sister Magdalene's office, and gently tapped on the door.

"Come in," a voice called from within.

Molly eased the door open and saw Mother Superior seated behind her desk.

Sister Magdalene rose to her feet when she saw who it was, a look of astonishment on her face.

"My goodness me! Hullo, Molly! Come in, come in. What a lovely surprise to see you. Please take a seat… Molly, are feeling all right? You look worried. Has something happened to Thomas? He looked very robust the last time I saw him."

Mother Superior was puzzled. Molly, whom she knew well, was obviously upset about something.

"Thomas is fine, Sister Magdalene. I am not here about Thomas. No, I am here to speak to you about something else."

African etiquette normally dictated a good few minutes enquiring about the health and well- being of family, friends etc before coming to the hub of the reason behind a visit. Molly dispensed with these formalities and came straight to the point, which alarmed Mother Superior even more.

"Sister Magdalene, you spoke to Boss Angus on the phone this morning. I answered the phone when you rang."

Mother Superior nodded.

Molly continued. "The telephone is in the hallway, next to the kitchen door. I was in the kitchen when Boss Angus spoke to you, so I could easily hear what he was saying without trying to listen."

Molly leant forward, her face serious as she emphasised to Mother Superior she wasn't in the habit of eavesdropping on other people's conversation.

"I understand what you are saying, Molly. I know you are the last person to pry into other people's business. Please go on."

"I heard Nurse Penny's name mentioned, Sister Magdalene, in a way that didn't make any sense. It seemed that Boss Angus was saying he and the dove love each other! Sister Magdalene, I have worked for Boss Angus for a long time and have always been loyal to him, but what he said to you and what he said to himself after he replaced the phone makes no sense. That is why I had to see you."

Molly stopped talking, as she cast her mind back to the morning.

Mother Superior broke in onto her thoughts.

"What did Boss Angus say?"

"After he put the phone down, he said, "I hope Clair is satisfied, I know I am.""

Mother Superior drew in a sharp breath.

"Boss Angus said that? Are you absolutely sure, Molly?"

"Yes, Sister Magdalene, those were his words. I don't understand, but I know something is wrong. Something bad is happening to our dove. I know I shouldn't say this, but I never felt Nurse Clair could be trusted. Nurse Penny loves Doctor Maynard, and I am sure Doctor Maynard loves the dove. Boss Angus has hated the good doctor ever since his wife died; you know everything about the tragedy, Sister Magdalene. Big trouble is deliberately being caused for our Nurse Penny."

Molly stopped talking as Sister Magdalene abruptly pushed her chair away from the desk and began pacing the floor.

"Could I have been so wrong in my judgement of character?" she muttered to herself. "Has Molly recognised Clair for the type of person she is but I didn't? I believed everything Clair told me, but I wouldn't even listen to Penny, who, at this very moment is on her way home. How could I have made such a hasty decision without finding out all the facts? What an old fool I've been!"

She stopped pacing and looked hard at the maid.

"Molly, you are absolutely certain you heard what you have told me?"

"Yes, Sister Magdalene. I would stake my life on it. Boss Angus does not love the dove. That is a lie. The dove loves Doctor Chris, not Boss Angus. I believe Nurse Clair is the one making trouble, and she has used the boss to get what she wants. I knew something was wrong when Nurse Clair visited Boss Angus on her own. I heard she told Nurse Penny and the doctor she had stomach pains. That is why she didn't go with them to the village that morning. She saw Boss Angus instead. I wish I had heard her talking to the boss, but I had to visit my sister who was ill. Nurse Clair has used the boss's anger against Doctor Chris for her own means to hurt our dove."

There was silence, then Mother Superior smiled at her old friend and said," you did right coming to me. I have made some very bad decisions I now need to make right. Take yourself to the dining room and get some refreshment, and Molly, please don't worry. You did the right thing coming to me. Have you a lift home?"

"Yes, David is taking me back."

"Good. Do not say anything to Boss Angus. I will make sure your name is not mentioned in whatever decisions I take."

"Thank you, Sister Magdalene. Boss Angus is a good man. Hatred and jealousy can cause good men to do bad things they wouldn't normally do."

Molly walked to the door, smiled her goodbye to Mother Superior and enjoyed a cup of tea with a clear conscience.

Mother Superior, however, was not so fortunate.

CHAPTER TWENTY TWO

One telephone call from Sister Magdalene and Penny's plane ticket to London awaited her at Entebbe airport. Within an hour of the devastating interview with Mother Superior, the nurse was seated in a land rover, her suitcases stowed in the luggage compartment.

Struggling to contain her tears whilst a cauldron of emotions boiled up inside, she cast a last look back at the place that had given her so much joy and satisfaction, and now so much heartache.

And I didn't even have time to say goodbye to Ruth and the baby. What a ruthless streak there is in Sister Magdalene. No wonder Idi Amin took fright.

Penny slumped back in her seat; despair flowing over her knowing she had no chance to prove her innocence. She remembered with dismay, the disgust and anguish in Chris's voice, the hurt in his eyes as he said those hideous things to her.

Oh Chris, how could anything as beautiful as our love turn so horribly wrong? How incredibly naive of me to think Clair would just accept our love. I know I walked away from Jane and Michael, but Clair's not me. She had her own agenda and although I admit her lies were diabolical, in some strange way I understand her actions.

Dry, bone- shaking sobs wracked her body and she gave in to the despair overwhelming her.

Joseph looked into his rear view mirror and his heart melted in pity at the sight of the dove so sad and beaten.

What terrible thing has happened for Nurse Penny to leave The Haven like this? We will miss her very much. She has found a way into all of our hearts. I wish there was something I could do to help her, but Mother Superior's orders were not to be argued with. Straight to the airport, no stopping on the way and make sure Nurse Penny gets on the plane for Johannesburg International Airport where she will catch a connecting flight to England.

And that's exactly what Joseph did, little knowing how frantically Mother Superior tried phoning the airport to leave a message cancelling Penny's ticket and for him to bring the nurse back to The Haven.

But a telegraph pole hit by lightening foiled her attempts to get through and the driver duly escorted a zombie like Penny to passport control where other passengers bound for South Africa swallowed her up.

Penny sat in the departure lounge at Johannesburg International Airport, a cup of coffee going cold on the table in front of her as she contemplated a bleak future without her beloved doctor. She remembered the last time she'd sat here, sipping coffee and eating koeksuisters, full of excitement at the new life extending in front of her, a life that had now ended in betrayal of the worst kind.

She heard her flight number over the tannoy system, and, without a backward glance, picked up her hand luggage and followed the stream of passengers boarding the plane to Heathrow, London.

"Good bye Chris," she whispered. "I will always love you."

CHAPTER TWENTY THREE

Back at The Haven, Sister Magdalene trembled in a state of impatience.

Furious at herself for not being able to stop Penny at Entebbe Airport, she'd tried contacting Doctor Maynard at Jinja but failed on that score as well, not knowing he was on a sight seeing tour with the ever-clinging Clair, and had turned off his mobile phone.

Feelings of frustration and helplessness grew until screaming out loud seemed the only answer!

"You stupid old fool," the nun berated herself out loud as she paced the floor of her office.

"What's that saying? Act in haste and repent at leisure. How am I to get the truth to come out and make things right. Now, just calm down and think. I need Clair to own up to what she has done. I need Angus to admit he was in cahoots with her, and I need Chris to be present at both confessions, but how to do that without bringing Molly into it?"

A germ of an idea entered her head, which she immediately dismissed out of hand. It involved an innocent child, but the idea refused to go away.

"Maybe a miracle will happen. Lord knows I need one, and He's never let me down in all the years I have served Him."

After much soul searching, Mother Superior decided to take action, and to leave the details to the Lord she had served so faithfully for most of her life.

She called Thomas and asked him to bring his land rover to the driveway.

"I need to go to Jinja immediately. Please be as quick as you can."

Thomas hurried away and within five minutes, was waiting for Sister Magdalene to finish talking to Sister Mary, her second in command. He then helped the nun into the back of the vehicle.

"Straight to Jinja, please. Once there, I will give you directions."

As Thomas concentrated on his driving, Sister Magdalene contemplated her next move. She knew where baby Angus was living. Doctor Maynard had informed her who was fostering the child until Angus came to his senses. The nun knew the Rivas family well, and always thought Chris had made a good choice for foster parents.

The miles sped past and by four in the afternoon, Thomas drew up outside the Rivas household.

"Come in with me Thomas. I'm sure Madam Rivas will offer you some refreshment."

"With all respect, Sister Magdalene, I would like to take this opportunity to visit my sister. She works at the municipal building and I have not seen her for over a month."

"That's fine. You do that. I may be here a while."

Mother Superior walked along the garden path and up the short flight of steps to the entrance of the house, and after saying a short prayer under her breath, used the knocker.

Rosina opened the door, and was surprised to see the old nun standing there.

"Mother Superior! How nice to see you! Madam Rivas is in the lounge writing letters. She will be so pleased you have visited. Please, come in," and the maid ushered the nun into the lounge.

Madam Rivas advanced upon Mother Superior, arms outstretched, a warm welcome in the beaming smile on her face.

"Mother Superior, how lovely of you to visit," and she hugged the diminutive figure of the nun.

"Please sit down. Are you thirsty? Can I offer you any refreshment?"

"Fruit juice would be lovely," and Sister Magdalene settled herself in her chair, whilst Madam Rivas organised the drinks.

Within minutes, the two women were sipping ice-cold mango juice with a dash of pure orange.

Madam Rivas spoke. "You know it's always a pleasure to see you, Sister Magdalene, but I get the impression this is not just a social visit. You look troubled. Is there anything I can do to help?"

"You have always been perceptive," smiled the nun. "Yes, I am concerned about a wrong doing that has to be put right, and although I have no idea as to whether you can help me or not, there are a few questions I would like to ask, but first, how is baby Angus?"

Madam Rivas smiled. "He is beautiful, such a lovely child, and clever! Oh, Sister Magdalene, how I wish Angus would just take one look at his son. That's all that's needed for him to see at a glance the baby is his. They are like two peas in a pod. See what I mean?" and she turned to face Rosina carrying the baby into the lounge.

Mother Superior held her arms out to the infant, marvelling at the deep copper colour of his thick curls and the facial features revealing an unmistakable likeness to his father. Baby Angus gurgled happily at the nun whose eyes misted over on seeing the baby's mother looking at her through her offspring's eyes. Yes, mother and father could clearly be seen in this baby's make up.

"The resemblance is marked, and you have done a wonderful job, Madam Rivas. How I pray, one day, Angus will come to his senses. Which brings me to my next question."

The nun rearranged her habit as she formulated the question in her mind.

"I believe you had a visit from one of my nurses? Penny Whickam is her name."

"Oh yes! What a lovely person. As soon as Penny saw baby Angus, she just wanted to get father and son together. She knew once Angus saw the child, he would have no more doubts."

Penny spoke the truth, thought Mother Superior. *I truly believe if Angus can be persuaded to see the baby, somehow all the facts will surface and the lies be exposed.*

CHAPTER TWENTY FOUR

Angus heard Molly clatter down the veranda steps.

He relit his pipe and sat contentedly, puffing away, reliving Chris's disenchantment with his beloved nurse, Clair's triumphant boasting and his own satisfaction at getting back at his nemesis.

But something happened to disturb his reverie.

Whilst picturing the doctor's distress, Penny's image covered Chris's face, the dove's beautiful, innocent eyes looking at him, huge question marks asking why? Why? What have I done to justify this treatment?

"Ach, I'm not deliberately getting at you, Penny," said Angus aloud. "You're just the means to an end. I'm sorry you had to get hurt, but that's what happens when you get mixed up with a bastard like bloody Doctor Maynard."

Angus pushed Penny to one side and replayed the scene he'd witnessed between Chris and the nurse. But his enjoyment at seeing Chris shaking with disgust and anger weakened as Penny's face appeared in the foreground, again with huge question marks in those beautiful eyes asking why? Why? But this time, accompanied with a forgiving smile, as she reached out a hand, placing it gently on his arm, her calm voice saying, "Let go of your bitterness and hatred, Angus. You must start living, not just existing. You have a son that needs his father."

"NO!"

Angus jumped to his feet, only then realising Cindy had rested her paw on his arm. The dog ran down the steps barking loudly and disappeared into the garden as the plantation owner stormed up and down the veranda, shaking his head violently to dislodge Penny's face. But she wouldn't go away.

He conjured up Clair, believing her arrogance and forceful personality would totally swamp the dove's gentleness.

Still Penny's image came to the fore, the word baby, baby, baby now cooing out of her mouth.

Angus grabbed his head, clutching it between his hands as though to squeeze out Penny's face.

"NO! NO!" he shouted. "Go away. You served your purpose, now go away!"

He grabbed his pipe, stuffing it furiously with tobacco, willing Penny's features to disappear, desperately wanting the triumphant feeling of revenge and justice to flood his being again.

It worked. Penny's image faded.

Angus sank back in his chair, struck a match and applied the lighted flame to the tobacco. Clouds of smoke emanated from the pipe, and he contemplated the whirls of patterns spiralling up into the air. A feeling of lassitude swept over him, numbing him, dragging at his defences, making him vulnerable to the one image appearing out of the whirls capable of completely disarming the Scotsman.

Staring at him, her eyes full of love and compassion, was his wife, his beautiful Lisa, her lips mouthing I love you as her likeness grew ever larger until Angus realised it wasn't only his wife he was looking at, but also his conscience. The anger, hatred and bitterness buried deep in his soul for so long, now escaped at a startling rate until, with a deep shudder, he fell to his knees sobbing uncontrollably.

With the sobbing came release, blissful, heavenly release from all things dire.

He felt cleansed throughout his body. The overpowering grief clouding his mind and judgement was gone. He knew he could look to the future. His wife had set him free. The dove had set him free.

"The boy is Lisa's child. The least I can do for my Lisa is take responsibility for her child, even though Chris is the father."

Galvanised into action by the free soaring of his spirit, the sensation of Lisa beside him, holding his hand, warmth flowing from her touch melting a frozen heart that now raced with life, the Scotsman rushed down the veranda steps to his land rover, intent on getting to Jinja as fast as possible...

... Angus lifted his hand to knock on the door of the Rivas household, and then slowly lowered it again.

I can't do this. What right have I to turn up demanding to see the boy? The child I've refused to have anything to do with, for over a year. They would have every reason to chase me off the property, and I wouldn't blame them. The first thought they'll have is I've come to cause trouble.

The plantation owner turned away from the house and lifted his eyes heavenward.

Heavy rain clouds gathered over Jinja from the west, flashes of lightening darting from one to another, illuminating extraordinary shapes sculptured by the wind. His mind reverted back to the day Lisa left to see Chris, a day like today, and how his unfounded jealousy and pride had prevented him from going with his wife, his Lisa, who felt concern and compassion for everybody who touched her life. If he had gone with her, would she still be alive today? That question had tormented him for over a year. He would never know the answer, but he could do the right thing now, and acknowledge Lisa's child as his own, even if it wasn't the case. It would be the right thing to do.

Thunder vibrated through his body. It was Lisa giving him the courage to face whatever consequences were waiting behind the door. He turned, and knocked loudly, his heart pounding, causing him to breathe in short rapid breaths.

The door opened, and there stood Madam Rivas. She stared at Angus, flabbergasted.

"Good afternoon, Madam Rivas. Please forgive me for turning up on your door step unannounced, but, I had to come."

"Angus! Oh, Angus! Come in, come in. How lovely to see you. I'm so sorry! It was such a surprise to see you standing there," and the lady of the house ushered the Scotsman into the lounge.

Mother Superior stood, her arms outstretched to welcome the prodigal son.

"Sister Magdalene! I didn't expect to see you here," and the plantation owner strode over to the diminutive nun, and hugged her tenderly.

"I've missed you Angus."

"I've missed you too. And I am sorry. That telephone conversation. It was all a lie, but somehow I believe you know that already."

The nun nodded.

"It's good you are here, Angus. There are issues needing clarity, issues I believe only you are able to make clear. However first things first."

Madam Rivas, after a brief, forgivable lapse, turned on hostess mode.

She invited Angus to take a seat and offered him refreshment.

"No thank you, Madam Rivas. I realise I'm the last person you expected to see, but, I had to come. I have to see the boy. I would understand if you've misgivings but it's really important I see him. For Lisa's sake." His voice trailed away, courage deserting him.

"Angus! Nothing would please me more. We've been praying for this moment for so long, haven't we Sister Magdalene?"

Mother Superior leant forward and clasped the plantation owner's hands between her own. "You are doing the right thing, Angus, and I promise, you won't be disappointed."

Madam Rivas had disappeared. Then she was standing in the doorway, holding the baby, who looked inquisitively at this stranger sitting next to the lady who always made him laugh.

Angus rose to his feet, eyes devouring the child, a replica of himself as a baby; the same copper colour hair, the wide, slightly lopsided grin with the suggestion of a dimple in the right cheek. Even at this young age, the nose was showing signs of the well- formed appendage it would become in later years.

Then baby Angus did something astonishing, taking everyone by surprise.

He stretched out his arms towards his father, straining against Madam Rivas, who looked in amazement at Mother Superior, and then walked over to the stunned visitor.

"He wants his father to hold him," and before Angus could do or say anything, put the baby in his arms and then walked away.

Angus carefully held the baby against his chest. He felt the child cuddle up against his body and nuzzle his forehead into the nape of his father's neck. The unique fragrance of a freshly bathed baby wafted into his nose and he wanted to savour that aroma forever. Tears threatened to spill over, as he gently lowered himself back into his chair. The baby stirred and sat upright, gazing directly into his father's eyes.

Angus returned the look, and time stood still.

His heart pounded as emotions rushed to the fore; any remnants of rage, hostility and overwhelming guilt were instantaneously replaced with a deep and enduring love.

For there was his Lisa, looking back at him, her eyes radiating love and forgiveness.

"I will always be with you, my darling. I live on in our son, so each step he takes with you on the adventure called life, I shall be there also. Be the father to our son I know you can be, my love."

Then the moment ended, and the baby smiled and gurgled, his hands waving in excitement as he tried to jump up and down on his father's lap.

CHAPTER TWENTY FIVE

It was six pm at the Rivas household.

In the dining room, the host and hostess sat at opposing ends of the dining table, Clair and Chris next to each other and Sister Magdalene opposite the doctor, the seat beside her empty, but the table setting laid.

Clair, somewhat stunned at seeing Mother Superior talking with Madam Rivas when she and Chris arrived for dinner, covered her confusion well, and greeted the nun with composure. After all, she had accomplished the first half of her plan to be rid of Penny, and was basking in the glow of success. Now the second half was well in her grasp. She knew Chris needed more time in her company. All memories of Penny would then disappear forever, and the gorgeous doctor would know all about true love once he really got to know her.

Admittedly, the day hadn't gone totally according to plan, but Clair wasn't worried.

He just needs to relax, and as I see wine on the table. That augurs well for later on tonight. A couple of glasses, my darling, and you will be putty in my hands. I'll mould you exactly how I want you to be, and tingling with anticipation, she smiled at the doctor, but he refused to look her way. Intense feelings of aggravation continually rose in him at the proprietor way Clair grabbed his arm and hand.

Mother Superior noticed this with a great deal of satisfaction.

And then came the bolt out of the blue.

Standing at the threshold of the dining room surveying the scene stood Angus McFadden, having left his sleeping son in the nursery.

Clair felt fear and apprehension shoot through her body.

Angus was the last person she expected to see in this house. She forced a welcoming smile on her face and greeted her accomplice with as much warmth as she could muster.

Then common sense took over.

No reason for Angus not to be here. After all, the white and Indian community in Jinja is not that big. Angus has been invited to dinner the same way Chris and myself were. But I wonder how Chris is taking it?

The doctor sat thunderstruck.

Bewilderment and then suspicion crossed his mind in rapid succession. The memory of Penny locked in a passionate embrace with this man flooded his brain, tormenting his very being. It took all of his self- control not to attack the person who had destroyed his life. The thought of eating food in his presence made him feel physically sick. Rivas knew about the long running feud between the two of them. What was he thinking, inviting both of them to dinner at the same time? Was he looking for trouble? It didn't make any sense!

He looked at Mother Superior in consternation.

She smiled at him reassuringly and said, "Everything will soon make sense, Chris."

Madam Rivas invited Angus to the dining table.

"A place is set for you next to Sister Magdalene."

Mother Superior smiled at the plantation owner as he sat down beside her.

All the main players are here, all except Penny, which is unfortunate, but who knows, that may prove to be a good thing, thought the nun, as she broke a bread roll in half.

She looked again at Angus.

His spirit is lighter, the anger and bitterness has left him. He's ready to live again. Good can come out of something bad, and I believe this is the time when I shall be experiencing such an occasion. After all, one miracle has already come to pass.

Clair, meanwhile, was in turmoil.

She also saw the difference in Angus and didn't like it at all.

She cast warning glances at him but he chose to ignore her as he sipped the wine Rivas had poured.

"This is good stock, Rivas."

"Glad you like it, Angus. Imported from South Africa. Best vintage out of the Stellenbosch wineries. Let me give you a refill."

Dinner was served; dessert eaten and coffee drank during which small talk made up the conversation, although Chris said very little. Clair tried to put on a good show, attempting to be witty and amusing but felt instead she was swimming in molasses, slowly sinking deeper with each stroke.

Finally, the meal came to an end, a welcome relief for several of the guests.

Silence ensued for a moment, then Angus rose to his feet, and with a quick clearing of his throat, began speaking.

"Thank you Rivas and your delightful wife for the warm welcome you have given me. I know I don't deserve it, but nevertheless, you still extended it to me."

He paused and looked at each guest in turn, focusing last on the doctor, forcing him to meet his eyes before continuing.

"I am here tonight to right the terrible wrongs that have been done to you, Chris. The truth needs to be told, and now is the time to tell it."

He stopped talking, and looked hard at Clair.

Panic showed in her eyes as she silently implored Angus to keep quiet, but the coffee plantation owner was having none of it.

"I must tell the truth, Clair. Better for you, better for me. We can't live the rest of our lives based on lies."

Clair jumped to her feet, shouting, "No, Angus! Don't! You'll ruin everything!"

She looked wildly around the table.

"Don't listen to what he's saying. He's mad!" She turned to the doctor. "Chris! You know how much he hates you! He will always hate you, and he'll use anybody to fan that hate, including me. Angus used me, Chris, in his plan to get back at you. He'll tell you lies, I know he will!"

"Quiet! Sit down, Clair," commanded the doctor, understandably mystified.

Clair subsided and sank back in her chair.

Chris looked at his former friend. "I'm listening, Angus."

"Well, as you know, I made no secret of the fact I believed you had an affair with Lisa and you fathered a child with her. I was entirely wrong. I have seen my son. There is no doubt I am his father. Saying sorry is totally inadequate, I know, Chris, but I really am sorry for everything. I hope you will find it in your heart to forgive me. Yes, maybe I was mad, madden by grief so brutal it warped my mind, and I believed only the things I wanted to believe. I had to blame you, Chris, for Lisa's death. It was the only way I could live with my overwhelming guilt."

Angus pushed his chair away from the table and paced the room.

"Then Clair came on the scene. She'd sensed the antagonism between us the first time you, Penny and Clair visited the plantation. The next morning, she arrived on my door step, alone."

"The next morning? Stop there a minute, Angus, if you don't mind?"

Doctor Maynard looked at Clair, sitting with her head bent, black hair shielding her face.

"Is that right, Clair? The morning you said you had severe stomach cramps. Was that the morning you went to see Angus?"

"Yes," she whispered.

Chris stared at the nurse for a moment and then turned his attention back to Angus.

"Please continue."

"I wanted to hurt you badly. I detested you so much I was determined on ruining your life. I saw how much you love Penny, as much, I believe, as I loved my Lisa. When Clair came up with this scheme to disgrace Penny in your eyes because she hated her, and wanted you so badly, I believed this was the answer to my prayers. At last I could do to you what I thought you had done to me; destroy your life by removing the one person that meant everything to you."

He shook his head. "What was I thinking?"

Clair jumped to her feet again. "It's not true, Chris! Angus is lying! He's the one who suggested the whole thing. I said no! I didn't want to get involved."

"I don't believe that's quite correct," interrupted Sister Magdalene. "Please excuse me for butting in Angus, but Clair, have you forgotten the part I played in your wicked scheme? Have you forgotten the stories you told me about Penny being frightened of Doctor Maynard and accusing him of sexual harassment and even being fired from her job if she didn't do what he wanted?"

The nun shook her head in disbelief.

"How gullible I was to believe you, but how incredibly convincing you were."

The nun looked at Chris, his face severe and unyielding, sitting as still as stone.

"Please forgive this foolish old lady for the distress I've made you suffer. I still find it hard to believe how I was so taken in by Clair."

She turned to the nurse.

"You have missed your vocation, my dear. The stage is where you should be, deceiving audiences with your acting abilities, rather than misleading those people who were your friends. Penny only ever had good things to say about you. Not once have I heard her say anything unkind about anybody. She truly deserves her name the dove. I pray she will find it in her heart to forgive the injustices done to her."

Poor Doctor Maynard.

Sickened and disgusted at the way his love had been treated, he covered his face with his hands, not wanting to look at anyone. His defenceless dove, beaten and trodden to the ground by people she trusted and loved, friends who should have known better, but were too quick to believe the worst of her, including himself. Yes. He was as responsible as everyone else. He didn't give Penny any chances to explain. He just condemned her outright.

He spoke to Mother Superior.

"Sister Magdalene, I'm just as guilty as you. I said unforgivable things to Penny."

He turned to the plantation owner.

"That embrace Angus? Was that a put up job?"

"Yes, I'm ashamed to say it was. I waited for Clair's signal. Remember she was in your office? She was standing behind you, Chris. Once she raised her arm, I grabbed Penny and kissed her, knowing you would be looking, and it worked. You were made to think Penny and I were an item, but it was all lies. Penny only has eyes for you, I know that. I just pray she'll forgive us all, and that you get her back. I am so very, very sorry."

"Well, I'm not!" cried Clair. "I can't stand that sanctimonious, simpering bitch who has you all under her spell. Can't you see what she's done? She's fooled you all. She's not the goody two shoes you think she is. She deserved everything she got." Clair grabbed Chris's arm. He shook her off as though she was an abhorrent insect.

"Don't touch me! Don't ever touch me again. In fact, don't ever come near me or speak to me, ever. What a despicable excuse for a woman you are. Penny is worth a million of you."

"But Chris! Chris! I did it all for you, my love. Penny doesn't love you, not the way I do. I'm the one to make you happy, not Penny. Please Chris, let me show you how much I love you, please," and Clair tried to grab the doctor's arm again.

"Get away from me! You say you love me? You have no idea of the meaning of the word. Penny knows what love is. In fact Penny is love. Her whole being is love, and I let her go, heaven help me," and Doctor Maynard sank back in his chair, head bowed, his body shaking with heart wrenching sobs.

Mother Superior put her arms around her favourite doctor's shoulders and hugged him.

"Go to her, Chris. The dove will forgive us, I know she will. Go to Penny, and bring her back to us."

The doctor took a long, shuddering breath.

"Yes. I must go to my darling Penny. Pray, Sister Magdalene, pray like you've never prayed before, that Penny will forgive us all for the terrible wrongs we've done to her."

He cast one last appalled look at Clair,

"Make sure you are gone before I return. I never want to see or hear you again."

He then turned to Angus.

"We'll talk when I get back. I'll look forward to seeing you with your son."

And the doctor strode out of the house, Clair's pleadings falling on deaf ears.

Chapter Twenty Six

Penny laid on her bed, a sodden handkerchief clutched in her right hand.

She slowly raised herself to her feet and walked dejectedly to the window.

The weather reflected her mood, rain beating against the window, rivulets of water cascading down the panes of glass, mirroring tears cascading down her face until there were no more to be shed.

I've heard of people dying of a broken heart, but I never believed it. Now I know it's true. A person can still be alive outwardly, but inside they are dead. I know that for a fact because that's how I'm feeling now. I am dead inside

She had lost everything; her job, her reputation, in fact her life, but above all she had lost the only person in the world she could love. She knew she would never love anyone the way she loved Chris.

Her mother's words still echoed in her head.

"But Penny! I don't understand! Why won't you tell me what happened? Why didn't you let us know you were coming home? Why are you so upset? Please, please tell me! What is going on?"

How could she say, "Mother, I've been accused of sexual harassment, lying, cheating and worse, and there's no way I can prove my innocence. I left Uganda too shocked to even fight for what's right. That's the type of pathetic daughter you have!"

No, Penny didn't tell her mother anything; apart from saying she'd been unhappy and wanted to come home.

And what an enormous lie that was, she berated herself, *but I had to tell my parents something,* and she remained staring unseeingly out of the window.

Movement down below in the street caught her attention.

A car had stopped at the front door of the house.

Penny moved away from the window.

Probably one of mother's friends popping in for a chat. Please mother, don't ask me to come down and be civil, I don't want to see or speak to anyone.

"Penny! Penny! Are you awake, love?"

Her mother's voice echoed up the stairs.

Penny laid on the bed, flat on her stomach and yanked a pillow over her head, willing her mother to go away.

She heard a knock on the bedroom door, but remained silent, hoping her mother would think she was sleeping.

The knocking became louder, then the door opened and her mother was standing there.

"Penny dear, there's someone to see you."

"Please mum, tell them I'm sleeping, or I've gone out or anything. I don't want to see anybody."

"Well," said a deep masculine voice. "And after I've travelled goodness knows how many thousands of miles to see you. I hoped my welcome would be a little warmer, although I know I don't deserve it"

Hesitation crept into his voice.

"Penny, please my darling, forgive me. I know what really happened. I know you never betrayed me. Angus confessed all, incriminating Clair, much to her fury. In some ways I'm sorry you weren't there to witness the whole thing yourself, but I can't forgive myself for not believing you. What an incredible fool I've been. Mother Superior is also full of recriminations. I have a letter from her for you to read. Please Penny, I love you so much. Can you find it in your heart to forgive me for being such a monster to you?"

Penny didn't move.

"This is a dream. I must be dreaming," she whispered, not wanting to do anything to disturb the overwhelming love she felt cover her like a warm blanket, the warmth finding its way into her chilled heart, feeling life flowing through her again.

Oh, if only this was for real, she thought to herself, eyes shut tightly, willing the dream to continue.

Then she felt a hand gently rest on her shoulder, and the oh so familiar thrill course through her body. She sat bolt upright, disbelief mingling with overwhelming joy as she saw the only person in the world who could make her life worth living again.

"Chris," she whispered, "Is it really you?"

"Oh yes, my girl, it really is me," and Doctor Chris Maynard lifted her into his arms and was holding his dove so tightly she knew wild horses couldn't drag them apart.

Penny's mum tactfully withdrew, but not before she heard this delightful doctor claiming her daughter's hand in marriage.

"Penny, my darling dove, please say you'll marry me and soon. I'm too scared to let you out of my sight. Life without you is too terrible to contemplate. Please, my darling, say you'll marry me," doubt creeping into his voice, knowing how he'd wronged her, wondering if she really would forgive him.

He needn't have worried.

Penny's beautiful eyes enveloped him with such love he knew her answer even before she shyly smiled and said, "Yes, my love. Please make me your wife."

Words became superfluous as the universal language of lovers took over.

Penny's mother, meanwhile, did a little jig at the bottom of the stairs.

"So, Penny will be marrying a doctor after all!"

Printed in the United States
By Bookmasters